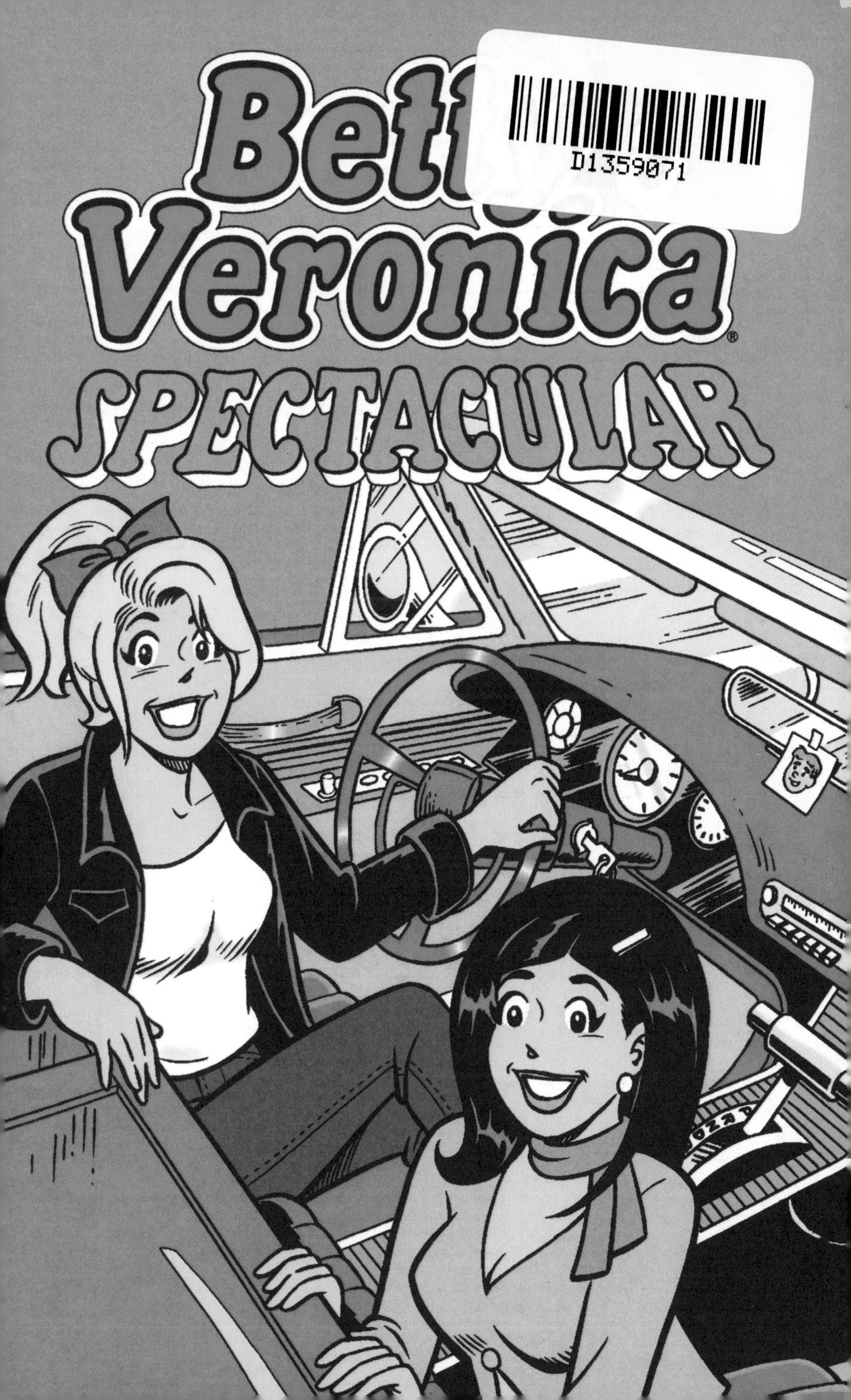
Veronica
SPECTACULAR

Printed in USA. First Printing. ISBN: 978-1-68255-825-6

WRITTEN BY

Dan Parent, Bill Golliher, George Gladir,
Frank Doyle, Mike Pellowski, Hal Smith,
Barbara Slate & Kathleen Web

ART BY

Dan DeCarlo, Dan Parent, Jeff Shultz,
Rex Lindsey, Mike Worley, Stan Goldberg, Alison Flood,
Henry Scarpelli, Mike Esposito, Mark Brewer,
Jon D'Agostino, Bill Yoshida, Rudy Lapick,
Barry Grossman, Nanci Dakesian & Frank Gagliardo

Betty & Veronica® SPECTACULAR

TABLE OF CONTENTS

Betty & Veronica SPECTACULAR

Welcome back to this second SPECTACULAR collection of some of Betty and Veronica's most hilarious and high-fashion moments! *Betty & Veronica Spectacular* showcased that Betty and Veronica aren't just fashionable friends who just so happen to fight over the same freckle-faced boy, but that they are two strong ladies who can maintain their own series. And, most importantly, it demonstrated just how funny stories featuring the two BFFs can be! This collection puts the emphasis on stories jam-packed with humor—be it slapstick, parody or just good old-fashioned fun! In this volume you'll find Betty and Veronica causing hijinks in unlikely settings like hospitals, home ec, and even atop a mountain. From the girls crashing fancy parties to having an out-of-this-world adventure to just clowning around, you're in for non-stop entertainment. Plus, a few special appearances from everyone's other favorite red-head and Betty & Veronica's nemesis, Cheryl Blossom!

Betty and Veronica in ACHES & PAINS (IN THE NECK!)

Story: Dan Parent Pencils: Dan DeCarlo & Dan Parent
Inks: Alison Flood Letters: Bill Yoshida Colors: Barry Grossman

Originally printed in BETTY & VERONICA SPECTACULAR #12, JANUARY 1995

SHE PASSED OUT!
SOMEONE GET HELP!

SO...
BETTY'S SUFFERING FROM *EXHAUSTION!* SHE'S BEEN OVER-DOING IT!
I KNEW SHE TOOK ON TOO MUCH!

CAN I GO HOME NOW?
ABSOLUTELY NOT! YOU'RE GOING TO BE HERE SEVERAL DAYS AT LEAST! WE'VE GOT LOTS OF TESTS TO DO!

AND AT LEAST THAT WAY YOU'LL GET SOME *REST!*
WELL, I SUPPOSE, IF I HAVE TO!

LET ME IN! I *MUST* SEE HER!
SO WHO'S *STOPPIN'* YA?

BETTY, DARLING, MY BEST FRIEND! DO YOU HAVE ANY FINAL REQUESTS?
YES! BUT I'M SURE YOU'D STILL BE HERE!
2

UH - NO THANKS, RON! I'M FINE! I'VE JUST OVERDONE IT!
WELL, I'M HERE FOR YOU BETTY!

WELL, YOU COULD GET ME A MAGAZINE TO READ!
OOPS! SORRY! GOTTA GO! I'VE GOT A NAIL APPOINTMENT!

TOODLES!
AT LEAST SHE STOPPED BY!

SO...
WHAT'RE YOU GUYS MAKING? A PARADE FLOAT?
NO, A GIANT CARD FOR BETTY!
GET WELL SOON BETTY

YOU'VE GOT TO BE KIDDING!
IT'S THE LEAST WE COULD DO! WE ALL LOVE BETS!

WELL, SO DO I! I AM HER BEST FRIEND, YOU KNOW!
C'MON, LET'S BRING IT OVER!
3

GEE, THANKS, GUYS! IT'S WONDERFUL!
HEY, LOOK OUTSIDE!
GET WELL SOON BETTY

IT'S FROM VERONICA!
GET WELL SOON, BETTY, LOVE, RON
15

JUST A LITTLE SOMETHING I PLANNED!
YEAH, RIGHT! YOU'RE JUST TRYING TO OUTDO THE REST OF US!
HOSPITAL

NONSENSE! CAN I HELP IT IF I'M RICH AND CAN AFFORD IT? - AND I AM HER BEST FRIEND YOU KNOW!

A TRUE FRIEND DOESN'T COMPETE FOR ANOTHER FRIEND LIKE A CONTEST!
A TRUE FRIEND GIVES OF HER-SELF! HER TIME... HER EFFORT!

OH, YEAH! WELL! MAYBE I'LL JUST SHOW THEM ALL!
4

THE NEXT DAY...
I COULD USE SOME WATER!
I'LL BUZZ THE NURSE!
BZZZ

HERE YOU ARE, BETTY!
THANKS, VERONICA!

SPEWW!
COUGH, GAG... VERONICA!
THAT'S MY NAME! DON'T WEAR IT OUT! GIGGLE

HOW...
WHAT...
WHERE...
I DECIDED TO SHOW YOU WHAT A TRUE FRIEND I AM!

SO I VOLUNTEERED AS A CANDY STRIPER AFTER SCHOOL! I CAN HELP YOU AND GUIDE YOU BACK TO HEALTH!

YOU DON'T HAVE TO DO THIS, VERONICA!
NONSENSE! I INSIST!!
5

VERONICA! WHEEL THIS CART DOWN TO ROOM 17!
OKAY! I'LL BE BACK TO COMFORT YOU, BETTY!

HMPH! I'M ACTUALLY DOING REAL WORK! BETTY BETTER APPRECIATE THIS! I'LL RUB IT IN ONCE SHE'S BETTER!

WOW! WHAT A CUTE DOCTOR!

OH, NO! MY CART GOT AWAY!
IS THAT VERONICA? IT CAN'T BE!

YES, MIDGE, IT CAN!...AND IT IS!
KRASH!

I'D LIKE TO KNOW WHO GAVE HER THE CRAZY NOTION TO WORK HERE!
UH... I'M SORRY, BETTY!
TO BE CONTINUED
6

ACHES & PAINS
(IN THE NECK!)
PART 2
BETTY DREAMS PLEASANTLY OF HER FAVORITE TOPIC!
BETTY! I ADORE YOU! LET'S RUN OFF AND ELOPE!
DECISIONS! DECISIONS!

VERONICA! YOU CAN'T DO THIS!!
POOF!
SO MUCH FOR PLEASANT DREAMS!

I DON'T SEE WHY I CAN'T WEAR THIS!
WE MUST WEAR STANDARD UNIFORMS! NO "DESIGNER" STYLES!
7

SO I HAD MY TAILOR WHIP UP A MORE CHIC CANDY STRIPER LOOK! WHAT'S THE CRIME IN THAT?
TAKE IT OFF OR LEAVE!

SINCE I CAN'T ABANDON MY DEAR FRIEND, I'LL CONFORM!
DARN!

LATER...
VERONICA, I CAN FEED MYSELF!
LET ME DO IT, BETTY! IT'LL MAKE ME FEEL MORE HELPFUL!

OKAY! MMPH!
NOW EAT IT UP LIKE A BIG GIRL!

SPLOTCH!
WOW! THERE'S THAT CUTE DR. REYNOLDS! I'VE GOT TO GO SAY HI!

YOO HOO! DR. REYNOLDS!
MODERN MEDICINE MAY NOT RECOVER FROM HER...
8

WHERE'S VERONICA LODGE? I NEED HER IN THE LAUNDRY!
SHE WENT TO LUNCH 2½ HOURS AGO!

OH, NO! SHE'S CAUSING HAVOC AGAIN!
MISS LODGE! WHERE HAVE YOU BEEN?

I WENT SHOPPING DURING MY LUNCH HOUR!
DON'T YOU MEAN LUNCH DECADE?

VERY FUNNY! IT'S NOT LIKE YOU'RE PAYING ME!
YOU STILL HAVE DUTIES! GET GOING!

SO...
BETTY! YOU LOOK MORE EXHAUSTED THAN EVER!
IT'S VERONICA! I CAN'T REST THROUGH ALL HER ANTICS!

SHE'S MAKING ME A NERVOUS WRECK!
I'LL GET TO THE BOTTOM OF THIS!
9

SO YOU SEE, DOCTOR, VERONICA'S PRESENCE IS TIRING OUT BETTY EVEN MORE!
I'M GLAD YOU CAME TO ME... I'LL FIX THE SITUATION!

BETTY, DARLING! I'VE BEEN SWITCHED TO THE THIRD FLOOR!
OH, HOW SAD!

I'VE GOT TO SPREAD MY CARETAKING ELSEWHERE!
BUT I'LL LOOK IN ON YOU FROM TIME TO TIME!

WELL, THAT'LL BE DIFFICULT, SINCE I'M GOING HOME TODAY!
YOU ARE?

YES! I'M SUPPOSED TO STAY IN BED FOR TWO WEEKS, THOUGH!
GEE, WILL YOU BE OKAY WITHOUT ME?

I THINK I'LL SURVIVE! BUT REMEMBER... THERE ARE PEOPLE WHO NEED YOU!
YOU'RE RIGHT! I MUST CARRY ON!
10

AH, TRUE REST AND RELAXATION!
YOU'RE LOOKING LIKE MY OLD BETTY AGAIN!

DING! DONG!
HMM! WHO COULD THAT BE?

VERONICA!
I COULDN'T LEAVE BETTY IN A BIND! FLORENCE NIGHTINGALE LODGE IS HERE!

RON!
I QUIT THE HOSPITAL, BETTY! THE ONLY REASON I WAS THERE WAS BECAUSE OF YOU!

NOW, LET ME BE OF SERVICE TO YOU!
WELL, YOU CAN GET ME SOME JUICE, I GUESS!

OKAY! BUT FIRST, LET'S WATCH OUR SOAPS! THEY'RE ON NOW! OH, AND DID I TELL YOU ABOUT THAT CUTE DOCTOR?
I WONDER IF THE HOSPITAL WILL RE-ADMIT ME?
END

Betty and Veronica in HOME EC-LESS!

Story: Dan Parent Pencils: Dan DeCarlo & Dan Parent
Inks: Alison Flood Letters: Bill Yoshida Colors: Barry Grossman

Originally printed in BETTY & VERONICA SPECTACULAR #12, JANUARY 1995

SEE YOU LATER, RON!
LATER! I'M OFF TO THE SUPERMARKET!

GEE! WE DO HAVE ONE IN RIVERDALE, DON'T WE?
!

LATER...
THERE! I'VE GOT PLENTY OF FOOD FOR MY $ 25!
SPAGHETTI, GARLIC BREAD, SALAD AND CHOCOLATE CAKE FOR DESSERT!

YUCKY! THIS FOOD IS ALL SO... SO COMMON!
WHERE'S THE GOURMET SECTION?

AH, THERE IT IS!
EXCUSE ME! I'D LIKE $ 25 WORTH OF CAVIAR, PLEASE!
FRESH
GOURMET

HA! HA! HA!
GOOD ONE! WOULD YOU LIKE THAT IN A THIMBLE OR AN EYEDROPPER?
2

IN CLASS:
BETTY, THAT DINNER LOOKS SPLENDID!
ANOTHER A+ FOR YOU!

OKAY, VERONICA! LET'S SEE YOUR DINNER!
REMEMBER! SOME PEOPLE LIKE LIGHT DINNERS!

VOILA!
WHAT IS IT?
WHERE IS IT?

IT'S ON THE PLATE! IT'S CAVIAR! WITH A FILLING AND TASTY CRACKER!
VERONICA! THAT'S NOT A VERY PRACTICAL MEAL!

BUT IT'S MUCH MORE EXCITING THAN SOME BLAND CASSEROLE!
AND DESSERT WAS SUPPOSED TO BE INCLUDED!

OH, YES! HERE!
A TIC TAC! MY, HOW FILLING!
3

SORRY, VERONICA! YOU FAIL!
BUT IF I FAIL THIS, I FAIL FOR THE SEMESTER!
GRADE BOOK

I'M AFRAID SO!
PLEASE GIVE ME ANOTHER CHANCE-- PLEASE!

WELL, I DON'T KNOW...
AW, GIVE HER ANOTHER CHANCE, MS. COOKE! SHE'S DOMESTICALLY IMPAIRED!

WELL, I GUESS I COULD GIVE YOU ONE MORE CHANCE!
THANKS, MS. COOKE! YOU'RE A GEM!

BUT, REMEMBER, ONLY $25 ON FOOD!
OKAY! GOT IT!

SO:
OKAY! TODAY'S THE DAY FOR VERONICA'S MEAL, PART TWO!
4

LET'S SEE IT!
OKAY! FIRST WE START WITH CHICKEN CORDON BLEU WITH A DELICATE RICE BLEND!

IT SMELLS *HEAVENLY!*
THAT'S THE CAESAR SALAD DRESSING!

AND FOR DESSERT, STRAWBERRY TORTE!
I'M IMPRESSED, VERONICA! THIS IS AN A+ MEAL!

IT'S *AMAZING* WHAT THE CHEF I *HIRED* WHIPPED UP, FOR ONLY $ 25 !
WHAT? VERONICA! YOU WERE *ONLY* TO *SPEND* $25!
IT MUST'VE COST YOU A *FORTUNE* TO *HIRE* A CHEF!

YOU SAID $ 25 ON *FOOD. NOTHING* ABOUT OUTSIDE HELP!
I *DID* SAY THAT, DIDN'T I, CLASS?

I THINK SHE'S GOT YOU ON A *TECHNICALITY!*
THIS IS THE *BEST* $ 500 MEAL I EVER *PAID* $ 25 FOR!
END

Betty and Veronica in DRASTIC SURGERY

Story: Dan Parent Pencils: Dan DeCarlo & Dan Parent
Inks: Alison Flood Letters: Bill Yoshida Colors: Barry Grossman

Originally printed in BETTY & VERONICA SPECTACULAR #12, JANUARY 1995

YOU MEAN IT'S SOMETHING YOU'D *ACTUALLY* CONSIDER?

I KNOW THAT I'M A PERFECTLY *EXQUISITE CREATURE*, BUT, WHAT THE HEY!
A LITTLE NIP AND TUCK NEVER HURTS!

WELL, I THINK IT'S A *DRASTIC* THING FOR PEOPLE TO DO... *ESPECIALLY* TEENAGERS!

THIS COUNTRY'S TOO *IMAGE*-CONSCIOUS!
YOU CAN COME OFF YOUR SOAP-BOX NOW!

ANYTHING THAT MAKES SOMEONE LOOK GOOD WORKS FOR ME!
ALL RIGHT! SEE YOU LATER!

THE WEEKEND...
VERONICA! YOU'VE GOT A *DREADFUL* RASH ON YOUR FACE!
I THINK I'M *ALLERGIC* TO MY NEW PERFUME!
2

I'LL GET HER TO THE DOCTOR IMMEDIATELY!

SO:
MY GOODNESS! YOUR FACE!
RELAX, DEAR! IT'S NOT AS BAD AS IT LOOKS! IT'S JUST TO PREVENT SPREADING!
DING DONG

OH, ARCHIE! VERONICA CAN'T...
YIPES! WHAT HAPPENED?

I'LL TALK TO YOU LATER, ARCHIE!
THIS IS EMBARRASSING!

MONDAY MORNING AT SCHOOL...
HMM! VERONICA'S OUT SICK TODAY! SHE DIDN'T EVEN CALL TO TELL ME!
IT WAS WEIRD! I STOPPED BY YESTERDAY, AND HER FACE WAS COVERED WITH BANDAGES!

OH, NO! SHE COULDN'T... SHE WOULDN'T!
AND I PROBABLY PUT THE IDEA INTO HER HEAD!
3

AFTER SCHOOL:
RON, HOW COULD YOU? I GUESS IT'S TOO LATE NOW!
I JUST WANT YOU TO KNOW I'LL SUPPORT YOU EVEN IF I DON'T AGREE WITH YOU!

I'M HERE FOR YOU! AND REMEMBER, I'M YOUR FRIEND NO MATTER WHAT YOU LOOK LIKE!
?

I'LL CALL YOU LATER!
SHE FINALLY CRACKED! TOO BAD! SHE WAS A NICE GIRL!

SO:
HI, MRS. LODGE! IS VERONICA HOME?
NO, BETTY! SHE WENT BACK TO THE DOCTOR FOR MORE!

HELLO, BETTY?
I'VE GOT TO GET TO THE HOSPITAL! I MIGHT BE ABLE TO STOP HER THIS TIME!

THERE SHE IS AT ADMITTING! THANK GOODNESS!
VERONICA! STOP THE INSANITY!
ADMITTI
4

EXCUSE ME?
OH, MY GOSH! WHAT HAVE YOU DONE TO YOUR FACE?

I BEG YOUR PARDON!
I MEAN, IT'S OKAY, BUT YOUR OLD FACE WAS YOUNGER!

WHAT'S THIS? BETTY GETTING YELLED AT! THIS IS A FIRST!

WHAT'S UP, BETTY?
HUH?
VERONICA? BUT WHO IS...

YOUR MOM SAID YOU CAME FOR MORE... PLASTIC SURGERY!!
MORE LOTION FOR MY SKIN INFECTION!

I'M SO EMBARRASSED!
MAYBE YOU'D LIKE TO HIDE IN THESE BANDAGES!
END

Story: Dan Parent   Pencils: Dan DeCarlo & Dan Parent
Inks: Henry Scarpelli   Letters: Bill Yoshida   Colors: Barry Grossman

Originally printed in BETTY & VERONICA SPECTACULAR #13, FEBRUARY 1995

SOMEDAY WHEN I'M OLD AND GREY, I MAY WANT TO REMEMBER THINGS!
HMM! YOU'VE GOT A POINT!
Betty's DIARY

I'D HATE TO FORGET ABOUT SOME OF THE GREAT DESIGNER OUTFITS I'VE BOUGHT! MAYBE I'LL KEEP A DIARY, TOO!

THAT'S FINE, BUT YOU SHOULD FILL IT WITH YOUR FEELINGS, NOT WHAT YOU FIND AT THE MALL!

YOU DO IT YOUR WAY, I'LL DO IT MINE!
WHATEVER YOU SAY!

SOON:
I'VE GOT THIS BIG, BEAUTIFUL, JEWEL-PLATED DIARY...

AND I CAN'T THINK OF ANYTHING EXCITING TO PUT IN IT OTHER THAN MY LATEST PURCHASES!
2

BETTY WAS RIGHT! I NEED SOME EXCITING, PERSONAL REFLECTIONS IN HERE! NOW, WHAT DO I WRITE...

HEY! MAYBE I CAN GET SOME IDEAS FROM BETTY'S DIARY! ONLY I'VE GOT TO FIGURE OUT A WAY TO SNEAK A PEAK...

THE NEXT DAY...
I'LL BE READY IN A MINUTE, RON...
OH! YOU'D BETTER GET THAT!

YOUR DOORBELL JUST RANG.!!
WHAT? I DIDN'T HEAR ANYTHING!

IT DID? WELL, I'LL BE RIGHT BACK!
TAKE YOUR TIME!

AH, THERE'S THE KEY, JUST WHERE I SAW HER PUT IT! AND HERE'S THAT DIARY!
3

NOW FOR THE *READ* OF THE DAY!

HELLO!
OH, HI, LEROY! WHAT'S UP!
OH, NOTHING! WOULD YOU LIKE TO *BUY* SOME BOY SCOUT COOKIES?

SINCE WHEN DO BOY SCOUTS SELL COOKIES?
OH, ER... IT'S A *NEW* THING!

HMPH! SOMETHING IS UP!
HOLD ON, LEROY! I'LL GET SOME *MONEY*!

AH, HA! I *KNEW* YOU WERE UP TO SOMETHING!
GULP! I-I... WHATEVER DO YOU MEAN?

IF YOU WANT TO *READ* MY DIARY, JUST ASK!
HMPH! I DON'T *NEED* TO READ ANYONE'S DIARY!
4

COME, LEROY!
WHERE'S THE FIVE BUCKS YOU PROMISED ME?

SO...
HI, MUMSY! I'M BACK FROM SHOPPING!
OKAY! BETTY'S WAITING FOR YOU UPSTAIRS!

OH, THAT'S NICE! I...
OH, NO! SHE MIGHT LOOK AT MY...

DIARY!
HI, VERONICA! I CAN'T BELIEVE YOU WASTED SO MUCH MONEY ON THIS AND ONLY FILLED IT WITH A HALF-PAGE OF STUFF!
Veronica's DIARY

OF ALL THE NERVE! PEEKING IN MY DIARY!
WHAT ABOUT YOU PEEKING IN MY DIARY?

IT WAS SIMPLY RESEARCH!
LET'S FACE IT, RON, YOU'RE NOT A "DIARY" KIND OF GAL!
5

GRRRR! LIKE YOU'RE SOME DIARY EXPERT!
LOOK, RON!! "THE TRUE WORLD" IS ON!
THE TRUE WORLD
HEY! THAT'S THE SHOW THAT FILMS THE REAL LIVES OF YOUNG, HIP PEOPLE!
YEAH! FOR ALL OF US TO WATCH!
A REAL CAMERA FOLLOWS THEM AROUND AND CAPTURES THEIR EVERY MOVE!
I COULD NEVER ALLOW THAT! MY DIARY IS MY TRUE WORLD!
HMMM!

IT'S LIKE AN EGOCENTRIC WAY OF KEEPING A DIARY! IT'S LIKE SOMETHING YOU WOULD...

VERONICA! NO! DON'T EVEN THINK IT!
CONTINUED-6

Betty and Veronica
DIARY DAZE
PART II
HI, RON! HEY, WHAT'S THIS?
JUST IGNORE THEM! THEY'RE MY CAMERA CREW TO FILM MY "VIDEO DIARY"!
VIDEO DIARY?

RON HAS DECIDED TO MAKE A VIDEO DIARY, LIKE "THE TRUE WORLD"!
THAT'S RIGHT! AND YOU'LL ALL BE A PART OF IT!

I'LL BE FILMED 24 HOURS A DAY!
I WILL THEN EDIT IT INTO AN EXCITING VIDEO DIARY!
7

THAT SHOW, "THE TRUE WORLD," IS COOL!
JUST LIKE MY LIFE!

NOW, GANG, WHAT'S NEW?
--ER-UM!

ER-AH!
UM...
OH!

C'MON! DON'T BE CAMERA SHY!!
SPEAK UP!!!

BURP!
GIGGLE!
I NEED CLASSIER FRIENDS!

IN CLASS...
VERONICA! WHAT'S ALL THIS?
JUST MY FILM CREW!
8

I'M HANDING BACK YOUR TESTS, CLASS...
ER... YOU MAY NOT WANT TO FILM THIS, VERONICA!

NONSENSE I... WHAT? A "D"! HOW DID THIS HAPPEN?
I DEMAND AN EXPLANATION! I... ER...

I'LL JUST HAVE TO STUDY HARDER NEXT TIME!
I'LL HAVE TO EDIT OUT THAT LITTLE TANTRUM!

AFTER SCHOOL...
THEY CAN FILM HOURS OF ME TRYING ON DESIGNER OUTFITS!
THE CAMERA JUST LOVES ME!

I'LL JUST SWING AROUND AND...
EEK! MY DRESS IS CAUGHT, I...

RRIPP
CAMERAS OFF!!!
9

THAT WAS HUMILIATING! BUT I SHOULD HAVE LUCK AFTER A GOOD NIGHT'S SLEEP!

AT 3 A.M.!
OOH! MR. REDFORD... YOU SAY THE NICEST...
Z Z Z
SNORE
SNORE

HEY! WHAT'S GOING ON? DON'T I GET ANY PEACE?
SORRY! HEY, DID YOU KNOW YOU SNORE?

I WHAT?!? GET OUT! NOW!!
I'LL JUST HAVE TO EDIT THAT OUT, LATER!

THE NEXT DAY...
ARCHIE'S TAKING ME TO THE DANCE! A ROMANTIC EVENING IS AHEAD!
VERONICA! ARCHIE'S HERE!

ARCHIE! WHAT HAPPENED?!?
MY CAR BROKE DOWN! I HAD TO BRING MY BIKE!
10

BUT DON'T WORRY! YOU CAN RIDE ON THE HANDLEBARS! I'LL STEER!
ANOTHER MOMENT TO EDIT!

SOON...
VERONICA! IT'S BEEN THREE DAYS! YOU PROMISED TO GIVE ME A VIDEO DIARY PRESENTATION!
IT'S ALMOST READY!

NICE INTRO!
THANK YOU!
Veronica's
VIDEO DIARY

THAT'S ALL, FOLKS!
HUH?
WHERE'S ALL THAT FOOTAGE YOU SHOT?

IT WAS ALL SO EMBARRASSING! I KEPT EDITING THINGS OUT!
BEFORE I KNEW IT, I WAS DOWN TO 4 SECONDS OF A SHOW!

HAVE YOU LEARNED A LESSON, VERONICA?
I SURE HAVE! DIARIES ARE TOO MUCH HASSLE! I'LL STICK TO READING YOURS!
END

Story: Dan Parent Pencils: Dan DeCarlo & Dan Parent
Inks: Henry Scarpelli Letters: Bill Yoshida Colors: Barry Grossman

Originally printed in BETTY & VERONICA SPECTACULAR #13, FEBRUARY 1995

YOUR PARENTS LET YOU ORDER THEM?
WELL...
ONCE THEY SEE THEM, THEY'LL FALL IN LOVE WITH THEM!
WHY DID YOU DO THIS?
I THOUGHT OUR GROUNDS COULD USE A MORE WILD, COUNTRY LOOK! AND YOU KNOW HOW I HATE CAMPING!
...SO YOU BROUGHT THE WILDERNESS TO YOU!
EXACTLY!
AND JUST WHO WILL TAKE CARE OF THEM?
I THOUGHT YOU COULD HELP ME!
COULD YOU STAY OVER TONIGHT? WE CAN CHECK ON THEM 'TIL THEY ADJUST TO THEIR NEW SURROUNDINGS!
WELL... I GUESS SO!
2

THE AFTERNOON...
BETTY, IT'S REALLY SNOWING OUTSIDE!
CAN WE HOUSE THEM IN THE GARAGE UNTIL THE STORM IS OVER?

GOOD IDEA! LET'S GO ROUND THEM UP!
OH, HI, DADDY!
CATERING

WHAT'S ALL THIS?
TONIGHT'S OUR ANNUAL WINTER SOCIETY PARTY! DID YOU FORGET?

OH, OF COURSE NOT!
BETTY, WE'VE GOT TO GET THOSE REINDEER OUT OF HERE BEFORE THE PARTY BEGINS!

SO...
GIRLS? WHERE ARE YOU GOING WITH THE FOOD CART?
JUST TESTING OUT THE WHEELS FOR LATER, MOM!

THERE! WE'VE GOT THEM IN SAFELY!
NOW TO KEEP THEM HERE, QUIETLY!
3

THAT EVENING...
GUESTS ARE STARTING TO ARRIVE!
WE'VE GOT TO FEED THE DEER -- THEY MUST BE STARVED!

GIVE THEM THESE SWEDISH MEATBALLS!
OKAY!

WOULD MADAME CARE FOR A --
HMM... I COULD'VE SWORN...

EAT UP, BOYS! I'LL GET YOU MORE LATER!
I WANT MORE NOW!!

I SMELL LOTS OF GOOD EATS!
I'M TRYING TO TURN THIS ROUND THING, LIKE THAT BLONDE GIRL!

THERE! LET'S GO! I'M FAMISHED!
EEK!
WHAT ARE THEY?!
4

REINDEER? HOW? WHAT? WHERE?
THEY'RE EATING MY BAKED ALASKA!!

AH, A PLACE TO HANG MY COAT!
HUH?

HELP!
THE COAT RACK IS ATTACKING ME!
THIS EVENT WILL BE DESTROYED IN THE SOCIETY COLUMN!

WHO'S RESPONSIBLE FOR ALL THIS?
I THINK I HAVE A CLUE!

BECAUSE WE THINK THIS IS HILARIOUS!
FINALLY! SOME LIFE TO ONE OF THESE DULL SOCIETY PARTIES!

Y-YEAH? WE THOUGHT THIS WOULD BE A WACKY IDEA!
JUST LEAVE IT TO THEIR WACKY DAUGHTER!
The End

Betty and Veronica in CLOWNIN' AROUND!

Story: Bill Golliher Pencils: Dan Parent
Inks: Mike Esposito Letters: Bill Yoshida Colors: Frank Gagliardo

Originally printed in BETTY & VERONICA SPECTACULAR #14, APRIL 1995

LATER...
YOU GUYS SURE ARE FUNNY!
THAT'S WHAT WE CLOWNS DO! RIGHT, RON?!
HUH? YEAH! THAT'S US!
ABC

NOW I'LL MAKE BALLOON ANIMALS FOR EVERYBODY!
THAT GURNEY LOOKS COMFY!
OH, GOODY!

MAYBE I'LL STRETCH OUT A MINUTE WHILE LADY BOZO'S ENTERTAINING THE KIDS!

AHHH! THIS FEELS SO GOOD I...
ZZZ!
MAKE ME A GIRAFFE!
OKAY!

HEY, LOOK! SHE'S ASLEEP!
GRAB A SHEET! I'VE GOT AN IDEA!

NOW SHE LOOKS LIKE A STIFF CLOWN!
LET'S SNEAK HER DOWN THE HALL AND GIVE HER A SEND-OFF!
b Cc Dd Ee
2

QUICK! THE NURSES AREN'T LOOKING! LET'S GET HER IN THE ELEVATOR!
HEE! HEE!

THIS POOR GIRL, SHE SHOULD'VE KNOWN LIFE HAS ITS *UPS* AND *DOWNS*!
HEE! HEE!
CLANK!

I'M SO GLAD I WAS ABLE TO CONVINCE YOU TO COME TO THE HOSPITAL TO HAVE YOURSELF CHECKED OUT!
WELL, THESE PLACES ALWAYS SCARE ME!

I KNOW IT MAY SOUND SILLY, BUT I...
AAARGH!! WHAT'S THAT?!

AT THE NEXT STOP...
DING!
OH, NURSE!
GROAN

THERE'S SOME *BODY* ON YOUR ELEVATOR!
WELL OF COURSE THERE'S *SOMEBODY* ON IT! A LOT OF PEOPLE RIDE IT!
3

NO! I MEAN A BODY! AS IN "PUSHIN' UP DAISIES" OR "BOUGHT THE FARM"!
ARE YOU SURE?

ALL YOU COULD SEE WERE HIS BIG : CHOKE : SHOES!
I'LL CALL SOME BODY... ER... SOMEONE TO CHECK IT OUT!

THIS IS GOING TO BE SOME PARTY!
KEEP IT QUIET! THE HOSPITAL DIRECTOR CAN'T FIND OUT! WE'VE GOT TO SNEAK THIS STUFF UP TO OUR DEPARTMENT!

WHOOPS! I PUSHED SEVEN BY MISTAKE!
OH, WELL! WE'LL JUST HAVE A LITTLE STOP ALONG THE WAY!
HEY, LOOK!

A BODY!
I WONDER WHAT HE'S DOING HERE?

LET'S THANK THE HOSPITAL DIRECTOR FOR THOSE WORDS!
UH-OH! THE SEVENTH FLOOR IS WHERE THEY'RE DEDICATING THE NEW WING!
RIVERDALE MEMORIAL
CLAP! CLAP!
4

QUICK! LET'S HIDE BEHIND THIS GUY!
WATCH IT! YOU'RE PUSHING!

UH-OH!
WE'D BETTER GET OUT OF HERE PRONTO!
SQUEAK! SQUEAK!

AND NOW MR. HIRAM LODGE, WHOSE DONATION IS MAKING THIS CONSTRUCTION POSSIBLE!
?
SQUEAK! SQUEAK!

WHAT'S GOING ON HERE?!
WHO'S THAT?!
IT'S MOVING!

HI, DADDY! : YAWN: WHAT BRINGS YOU TO THE HOSPITAL?
VERONICA?!

VERONICA! THERE YOU ARE! WHAT HAPPENED?
DON'T ASK! IT'S A LONG STORY!
The End

Story: George Gladir Pencils: Jeff Shultz
Inks: Henry Scarpelli Letters: Bill Yoshida Colors: Barry Grossman

Originally printed in BETTY & VERONICA SPECTACULAR #14, APRIL 1995

Betty and Veronica in "NO COMMON SCENTS"

Story: Bill Golliher **Pencils:** Dan Parent
Inks: Mike Esposito **Letters:** Bill Yoshida **Colors:** Nanci Dakesian

Originally printed in BETTY & VERONICA SPECTACULAR #14, APRIL 1995

SOME OF RIVERDALE SOCIETY'S BIGGEST NAMES! ALL THE WELL-KNOWN DEBUTANTES!
WHY SUCH A HIGHBROW CROWD?!

WITH THE PRICE TAGS ON THESE PERFUMES, YOU WON'T BE SEEING THEM AT Q-MART! THESE GIRLS ARE THE ONES WHO CAN AFFORD THEM!
I GUESS I SHOULD BE HONORED TO BE HERE!

YOU?! WHAT ARE YOU DOING IN MY HOUSE?
JUST PASSING THROUGH!

I COLLECTED SOME ANTS FROM THAT BIG ANT HILL IN YOUR BACKYARD FOR MY ANT FARM!
SEE!
EEK!!

GET THOSE INSECTS AWAY FROM ME!
HEY! WHY DON'T YOU PICK ON SOMEONE YOUR OWN SIZE!
SLAP!

NOW TAKE YOUR BUGS AND GET OUT OF HERE BEFORE MY GUESTS ARRIVE!
COME, BETTY! LET'S GO GATHER THE REFRESH-MENTS!
2

OH, GREAT! SHE KNOCKED THE TOP OFF AND LET MY ANTS OUT!

HMMPH! IT SERVES HER RIGHT!
I'LL JUST FIND ME SOME MORE ANTS ELSEWHERE!

DON'T YOU THINK YOU WERE A LITTLE TOUGH ON JUGGY?
MAYBE! I'M JUST A LITTLE UPTIGHT ABOUT THE GUESTS I'M EXPECTING!

DING DONG!
THERE THEY ARE NOW! LET'S GO GREET THEM!
I SHOULD'VE PRACTICED MY CURTSEY!

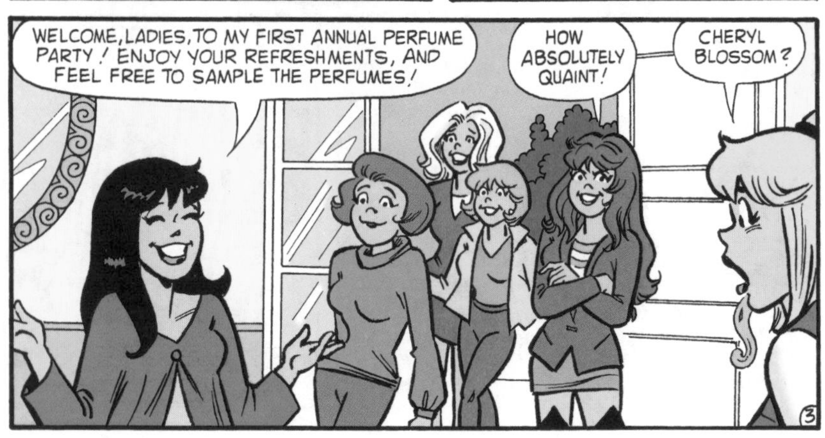
WELCOME, LADIES, TO MY FIRST ANNUAL PERFUME PARTY! ENJOY YOUR REFRESHMENTS, AND FEEL FREE TO SAMPLE THE PERFUMES!
HOW ABSOLUTELY QUAINT!
CHERYL BLOSSOM?
3

HELLO, GIRLS! IT LOOKS LIKE THIS SHOULD BE A FUN PARTY!
FUNNY, BUT I DON'T REMEMBER SENDING *YOU* AN INVITATION!

SINCE ANYONE WHO'S ANYONE FROM PEMBROOKE ACADEMY WAS INVITED, I JUST ASSUMED MY INVITE WAS LOST IN THE MAIL!
OH, YOU DID, DID YOU?

DON'T LET HER SPOIL IT FOR YOU! THE PARTY'S GOING WELL!
LET'S TRY THESE!

OH, THIS ONE SMELLS DIVINE!
TRY THIS ONE! IT'S SIMPLY BREATH-TAKING!

PHEW! THE COMBINED SMELL OF ALL THOSE SCENTS IS PRETTY POWERFUL!
IT'S SO SWEET-SMELLING!
ONLY TO YOUR UNCULTURED NOSE! TO US SOCIETY TYPES, IT'S A SUCCULENT NECTAR!
KOFF! KOFF!
4

OUCH! SOMETHING'S TICKLING ME!
WHAT *ARE* YOU TALKING ABOUT?!

THE *ANTS*! THEY MUST'VE ESCAPED WHEN YOU KNOCKED JUGHEAD'S ANT FARM OUT OF HIS HAND!
OH, NO! THEY'RE ON ME, TOO!

IT MUST BE THE SWEET SMELL OF THE PERFUMES ATTRACTING THEM!
OW!
EEK!

THIS IS SO EMBARRASSING! WHAT AM I GOING TO DO?
EEP!

SOON...
WHAT'S GOING ON, JUG?
I DON'T KNOW! VERONICA SAID SHE WAS HAVING A PERFUME TESTING PARTY...

...BUT IT LOOKS MORE LIKE SOME KIND OF *WILD* DANCE TO ME!
END

Story: Frank Doyle Pencils: Dan DeCarlo
Inks: Henry Scarpelli Letters: Bill Yoshida Colors: Barry Grossman

Originally printed in BETTY & VERONICA SPECTACULAR #15, JULY 1995

I COULD HANDLE BETTY, BUT THIS CHERYL BLOSSOM SCORES HEAVILY WITH ARCHIE!
SO WHAT?

YOU SCORE BROWNIE POINTS WITH ARCHIE EVERY TIME YOU BLINK YOUR EYES!
DADDY! I'M NOT TALKING BROWNIE POINTS!

CHERYL SCORES TOUCHDOWNS.!!
OH, MY!

PERHAPS I'M WORRYING NEEDLESSLY! AFTER ALL - WHAT'S SHE GOT THAT I HAVEN'T GOT?

ACK!
ARCHIE! THAT'S WHAT!
ROARR
2

I SAW THAT! THAT SNEAKY SNOB IS RUSTLING ON OUR TURF!!!
COULDN'T YOU JUST SPIT? AND, IF I WAS A BOY, I WOULD!

WELL, I'M GOING TO FIGHT FIRE WITH MONEY! WAIT'LL YOU SEE THE EXPENSIVE SWEATER I'M GOING TO BUY ARCHIE!
ROGUE MALE
EXCLUSIVE MENSWEAR

RON! YOU CAN'T BUY LOVE!
OH, HE'S NOT GOING TO KNOW IT'S FROM ME! I'M CREATING A SECRET LOVER!

ACME
DELIVERY SERVICE
CHERYL WILL GET JEALOUS AND DROP HIM LIKE A BAD HABIT!
ROGUE MALE
WE DELIVER ANYTHING ANYWHERE

SOMETIMES I THINK THAT'S WHAT HE'S ALWAYS BEEN!
YES, BUT HE'S ALWAYS BEEN OUR BAD HABIT!
ROGUE MALE

I WANT THIS DELIVERED ANONYMOUSLY! NOT EVEN A HINT ABOUT WHO SENT IT!
I'M THE BOSS HERE, LADY! I DON'T MAKE THE DELIVERIES!
WE DELIVER
3

ALL THAT MONEY, RON-- AND HE WON'T EVEN KNOW IT'S FROM YOU!
THAT'S NOT IMPORTANT THIS TIME!

THE MAIN THING IS THAT CHERYL WILL BE INSANELY JEALOUS AND SHE WON'T KNOW WHO SHE'S JEALOUS OF!

IT SOUNDS SUSPICIOUSLY LIKE A REGGIE MANTLE MANIPULATION!
WHAT'S THAT SUPPOSED TO MEAN?

I AM TOTALLY INNOCENT OF ANY "MANIPULATION"!
SORRY, GIRL! MY TONGUE GOT CAUGHT ON MY EYE TOOTH AND I COULDN'T SEE WHAT I WAS SAYING!

WELL, IF IT ISN'T "DIRTY POOL" CHAMP OF RIVERDALE! HAD TO CALL IN THE "A" TEAM, DIDN'T YOU?

ARE YOU IMPLYING THERE IS SOMEONE ELSE IN THE GAME?
AS IF YOU DIDN'T KNOW!
4

AT PEMBROOKE ACADEMY THEY TEACH *INTEGRITY!*
MISSED A LOT OF CLASSES, DIDN'T YOU?
CB
SCREEEE

(GIGGLE!) I DID IT! I OUTSMARTED HER WITH A *NON-EXISTENT* RIVAL!
SHE DID ACT LIKE A *LOSER!*

ARCHIE LOVES A MYSTERY! HE'LL BE INTRIGUED BY THE IDEA OF A *SECRET ADMIRER!*

AND, THEN AGAIN... MAYBE *NOT* SO SECRET!
HUH?

YOU SHOULD HAVE INSISTED THAT THE *BOSS* DELIVER THE SWEATER!
REMIND ME TO CHANGE MESSENGER SERVICES!
ACME DELIVERY
END

Betty and Veronica in "FOOD FLIP"

THAT WAS A GREAT PICNIC LUNCH, BETTY!
YOU SURE HAD A HEALTHY APPETITE, ARCHIE!
ICE BERG

Story: Mike Pellowski Pencils: Dan DeCarlo
Inks: Henry Scarpelli Letters: Bill Yoshida Colors: Barry Grossman

Originally printed in BETTY & VERONICA SPECTACULAR #16, OCTOBER 1995

AND SHE SAID HER DAD HAD A SURPRISE FOR HER!
I WONDER WHAT IT IS?

LET'S STOP BY HER HOUSE ON THE WAY HOME!
OKAY! I PLANNED TO RETURN HER PICNIC BASKET ANYWAY!

AT RON'S HOUSE...
SMITHERS SAID SHE'S OUT IN THE YARD!
GO SLOW, BETTY! THAT HUGE LUNCH IS STILL SETTLING!

HEY! HI, GUYS!
SPRONG!
HUH ?

WHAT THE...

COME AROUND THE HEDGES AND SEE WHAT I GOT!
SPRUNG!
2

A TRAMPOLINE!
COOL BEANS!

THAT LOOKS LIKE FUN!
WHY DON'T YOU TRY IT, ARCHIEKINS?

SORRY YOU MISSED THE PICNIC, RON!
YEAH! I BET!

DID ARCHIE ENJOY IT?
THE WAY TO A MAN'S HEART IS THROUGH HIS STOMACH!
BOUNCE
BOUNCE
BOUNCE

HMPH! WELL, NOW THAT YOU'VE FED HIM, HE'LL JUMP AT THE CHANCE TO SPEND THE REST OF THE DAY WITH ME!

WHAT DO YOU MEAN?
THAT!
THIS IS NEAT!

YAHOO!!
WHUMP

SEE! HE'S FLIPPING OVER THE IDEA OF SPENDING THE AFTERNOON HERE!
SPRUNG!

CHECK IT OUT! I'M SUPERDUDE!
BOUNCE!

UP, UP AND AWAY!!
SPRONGG!

WHOA! A SONIC SPIN!
BOUNCE!
BOUNCE!
4

SEE? SO WHY DON'T YOU TODDLE ALONG, BETTY?
OKAY, BUT ARCHIE IS COMING WITH ME!

HEY, ARCHIE! LET'S GO OVER TO MY HOUSE FOR A SNACK!
GULP! F-FOOD! OOOOOH!
BOUNCE
BOUNCE
BOUNCE
BOUNCE

ARCHIEKINS, WOULDN'T YOU RATHER STAY HERE AND BOUNCE AROUND WITH ME?

ARCHIE! WHAT'S WRONG?
I'VE STOPPED BOUNCING, BUT WHAT'S INSIDE MY STOMACH HASN'T!

OVEREATING AND BOUNCING SURE DON'T MIX... OOOOOH!
BURP!
BURP!
RUMBLE!
GURGLE!
GURGLE!
RUMBLE!

I'VE GOT A MONSTER BELLY-ACHE! MY STOMACH FEELS LIKE A VOLCANO!
5

CAN WE GET YOU SOMETHING?
NO THANKS! I'D BETTER GO HOME AND LIE DOWN!
OKAY! I'LL GIVE BETTY A RIDE HOME!
GURGLE
GURGLE

I HOPE ARCHIE FEELS BETTER! WHAT SHOULD WE DO NOW?
HMMM? I'M KIND OF HUNGRY! I SKIPPED LUNCH!

ARE THERE ANY LEFTOVERS IN THE BASKET?
PLENTY! WHERE WOULD YOU LIKE TO EAT?

THE GROUND IS KIND OF HARD! HMMM -- HEY! I KNOW!

THIS IS REAL COMFY!
AND THE FOOD IS GOOD, TOO! BUT JUST DON'T BOUNCE!!
End

Story: Dan Parent Pencils: Dan DeCarlo & Dan Parent
Inks: Rudy Lapick Letters: Bill Yoshida Colors: Barry Grossman

Originally printed in BETTY & VERONICA SPECTACULAR #17, JANUARY 1996

OH, I DON'T KNOW! OPPOSITES ATTRACT, *RIGHT?*
I GUESS! THAT MUST BE WHY I FIND BETTY SO *INTRIGUING!*

REMEMBER! AFTER VERONICA LEAVES WITH ADAM, I'LL RUN INTO BETTY LATER!
...JUST TO DRIVE THE WEDGE BETWEEN HER AND RON A BIT WIDER!

THEN I *SPRING* INTO ACTION, RIGHT?
DOWN, BOY, DOWN!

YOU'LL *COMFORT* THE POOR GIRL 'TIL SHE MELTS IN YOUR ARMS!
I *LIKE* IT! I *LIKE* IT!

SO...
JUST ONE LOOK INTO "CHEZ SWEATER" AND I'LL BE *DONE!*
THEY ALWAYS HAVE THE MOST BEAUTIFUL THINGS!
CHEZ SWE TER

BOING!
WOW! AND THEY *HAVEN'T* STOPPED!
WHAT DO YOU SEE?

TAKE A LOOK!
HUBBA HUBBA!
HE'S LOOKIN' AT ME!!
I THINK YOU NEED GLASSES! HE LOOKED AT ME!
ALL THAT MONEY'S MADE YOU DELUSIONAL! HE LOOKED AT ME!!
OUTTA MY WAY!
I'LL OUTRACE YOU ANY DAY!
CHEZ SWEA
HEY, YOU...
WATCH IT, YOU...
CRASH!
3

MAY I HELP YOU UP?
YOU SURE CAN!

I'M BETTY!
I'M VERONICA!
I'M HONORED! MY NAME'S ADAM!

OUT SHOPPING FOR NEW CLOTHES, ADAM?
YES, BUT I SEE SOMETHING I LIKE MUCH BETTER!
WHAT COULD THAT BE?

THIS KNOCKOUT NAMED VERONICA! WOULD YOU JOIN ME FOR A SODA?
I'LL SEE YOU LATER, BETTY!

HEE, HEE!! YOU WIN SOME, YOU LOSE SOME!
THIS IS ROTTEN, RON! LEAVING ME HERE LIKE THIS!

HONESTLY, BETTY! YOU'VE GOTTEN ON MY LAST NERVE!
I NEVER WANT TO TALK TO YOU AGAIN!
HEY, AT LEAST THIS'LL FREE ME UP FOR ARCHIE!
4

WHAT'S THAT? ARCHIE'S NOT HOME?
NO! HE WENT OUT OF TOWN WITH HIS DAD TO ATTEND A FOOTBALL GAME THIS WEEKEND!

TOO BAD! 'BYE, MRS. ANDREWS!
MAYBE I'LL SEE WHO'S OVER AT POP'S!

LATER...
OH, CHERYL! WHAT BRINGS YOU HERE?
OH, I SAW YOU FROM MY CAR! YOU LOOKED SO DEJECTED!

WHAT'S IT TO YOU, ANYWAY?
I'D SWEAR YOU LOST YOUR BEST FRIEND!

GULP
OH, DEAR! IT LOOKS LIKE I HIT A NERVE!!

MAYBE YOU SHOULD BUTT OUT OF THIS!
I'M JUST TRYING TO TELL YOU, MAYBE YOU NEED A CHANGE!
5

YOU NEED A NEW SET OF FRIENDS! YOU OBVIOUSLY CAN'T TRUST THE ONES YOU HAVE!
YOU TALKING ABOUT FRIENDSHIP? HA!!

I KNOW WHAT I SEE! YOU TOWNIES CAN'T BE TRUSTED!
DO YOU REALLY KNOW VERONICA OR EVEN ARCHIE? WHAT ABOUT JUGHEAD?

YOU BETTER KEEP YOUR EYES OPEN, POLLYANNA!
YOU'RE MEAN, CHERYL! I DON'T HAVE TO TAKE THIS ANYMORE!
OP'S

EVERYTHING'S GOING ALONG AS PLANNED! VERONICA'S WITH ADAM, AND BETTY AND VERONICA AREN'T SPEAKING!

IT'S TIME FOR THE FINAL PHASE OF THE PLAN! OH, JASON...
YOU CALLED, SISTER DEAR?

IT'S TIME FOR ACTION! GO GET HER!
YOU GOT IT, BOSS!
CONTINUED
6

Betty and Veronica
PART TWO
BETTY! BETTY! WAIT UP!!
I DON'T WANT ANYTHING TO DO WITH YOU BLOSSOMS!

PLEASE, BETTY! MY SISTER'S A CREEP, BUT DON'T LET HER GET TO YOU! CAN'T WE TALK?
WELL, I SUPPOSE YOU MAY BE A LITTLE MORE COMPASSIONATE THAN YOUR SISTER!
JUST TELL OL' JASON YOUR PROBLEM!
HYUCK! THIS IS TOO FUNNY!
7

HE PLAYS A SWEET GUY SO CONVINCINGLY!
ENOUGH TO REEL BETTY IN!
?

AND NOW WITH ALL PARTIES OCCUPIED, ARCHIE'S MINE!
SKIP
SKIP

SO...
I CAN'T WAIT TO SEE THIS MOVIE!
IT'S MY PLEASURE, VERONICA!
NOW PLAYING

BETTY ALWAYS WANTED TO SEE THIS SHOW! TOO BAD I'M NOT HER FRIEND ANYMORE!
PITY!

HMM! THOSE CUFFLINKS! THAT INSIGNIA LOOKS FAMILIAR!
OH, UM, ... IT'S JUST A RETAIL STORE LOGO! LET'S GET OUR...
P

WAIT A MINUTE! THAT'S THE PEMBROOKE INSIGNIA!
YOU'RE FROM PEMBROOKE!
8

YOU *LIED* TO ME WHEN YOU SAID YOU LIVE IN PARIS!
WELL, I VISITED THERE ONCE!

PEMBROOKE MEANS *ONE* THING! CHERYL BLOSSOM!
AND TO THINK I LEFT POOR BETTY BEHIND!

WELL, IT'S *LATE!* LET'S CALL IT A NIGHT!
IT'S 3:00 IN THE AFTERNOON! AND YOU BETTER FILL ME IN ON *EVERYTHING!*

OR I'LL HAVE YOU PERSONALLY DISMEMBERED BY MOOSE MASON A.K.A. "THE PULVERIZER"!
I'LL TALK! I'LL TALK!

SO...
THERE! DO YOU FEEL BETTER, BETTY?
YOU KNOW I DO!

I THINK I SEE A DIFFERENT SIDE OF YOU, JASON!
AW, SHUCKS!
9

OH, BROTHER! HERE COME VERONICA AND ADAM!
UH, OH! SHE LOOKS MAD!

LET'S SPLIT! WE DON'T WANT TO TALK TO THAT TRAITOR!
BETTY!! WAIT!!!

BETTY! GUESS WHAT? ADAM WAS SET UP BY CHERYL!
AND JASON IS SUPPOSED TO REEL YOU IN!

WHAT? I DON'T KNOW WHAT YOU'RE...
DON'T EVEN TRY IT, BUSTER! ADAM TOLD ME THE WHOLE STORY!

AND SOON...
ALL RIGHT, YOU MAY BOTH LEAVE! DON'T EVER CROSS OUR PATHS AGAIN!
MAN, THEY'RE BRUTAL!

I THINK I KNOW WHERE WE CAN FIND CHERYL!
LET'S GO!
10

WHAT? HE'S NOT HOME?
NO, HE'S OUT OF TOWN!
DRATS!!
THIS WASN'T IN MY PLAN! I HATE WHEN THIS HAPPENS!
GRRRR!!
OUT OF MY WAY, WORLD... I'M FIT TO BE TIED!
MOVE IT, POOCHIE, OR I'LL...
EEEK!
SPLOOSH
LOOK, RON! OUR WORK'S CUT OUT FOR US, AMIGO!
GREAT! LET'S TAKE IN A MOVIE, FRIEND!
CENSORED
HEE HEE! CHUCKLE!
I GUESS WE LOSE THIS ROUND, HUH, SIS?
End

Story: Hal Smith Pencils: Dan DeCarlo
Inks: Mike Esposito Letters: Bill Yoshida Colors: Barry Grossman

Originally printed in BETTY & VERONICA SPECTACULAR #17, JANUARY 1996

WHY ARE YOU WEARING THOSE SHABBY CLOTHES AND THAT FRIGHT WIG?
I'M IN DISGUISE!

EVER SINCE MY PICTURE APPEARED IN THE PAPER WITH AN ARTICLE ON HOW ...

I'M ON THE COMMITTEE THAT WILL SELECT THE TALENT FOR THE RIVERDALE CENTENNIAL CELEBRATION!

I'VE BEEN HOUNDED BY TERRIBLE SINGERS, AND WORSE DANCERS!

THAT IS A GREAT DISGUISE!
ISN'T IT, THOUGH?

I LOOK LIKE THE KIND OF PERSON I WOULDN'T WANT TO BE SEEN WITH!
2

LET'S TEST MY DISGUISE AT THE MALL!
OKAY!

I EVEN RENTED THIS WRECK OF A CAR FROM A SCRAP DEALER!

EXCUSE ME, MISS...
ME?

MAY I LOOK IN YOUR BAG?

HOW COME THIS SECURITY GUARD LOOKED IN MY BAG AND NOT YOURS?

WELL, SOME PEOPLE JUDGE OTHERS ON THEIR APPEARANCE!
3

AND I GUESS YOU DIDN'T FIT HIS IDEA OF WHAT'S ACCEPTABLE!
COMICS

NOT ACCEPTABLE? I'M STILL ME!!
I KNOW...
RIVERD
MALL

IT'S NOT FAIR, BUT UNFORTUNATELY IT'S HUMAN NATURE!
IT'S STUPID, IS WHAT IT IS!

OH, NO! THE MOTOR STALLED!
RRR
CHUNK!!

MAYBE SOMEBODY WILL STOP TO HELP US!

LOOK AT THAT! A DOZEN CARS WHIZZED BY AND NOT ONE STOPPED!
4

I'LL HAVE A LOOK AT IT! MAYBE I CAN FIX IT!

HAVING TROUBLE?
LET ME HELP YOU!
I CAN FIX IT!
AARGH!

THIS IS A TERRIBLE CAR! I'LL DROP YOU AT YOUR PLACE AND GO GET MINE!
SPUT!
POP!
PING!

LATER...
HELLO?
BETTY, I'M IN JAIL!

THE POLICE THINK I STOLE MY CAR! I LEFT MY LICENSE IN MY BAG AT YOUR PLACE!
I'LL BRING IT RIGHT OVER!

AND BRING A CHANGE OF CLOTHES, I'M TIRED OF BEING A BAG LADY!
5

DON'T WORRY ABOUT DRIVING WITHOUT A LICENSE! IT WAS OBVIOUSLY AN ERROR!
I'LL GET YOUR CAR FROM THE IMPOUND LOT!

IT'S REALLY GREAT BEING ME AGAIN!

HERE ARE YOUR CAR KEYS!
THANK YOU!
DRIVE CARE-FULLY!

OH, MISS LODGE, ONE MORE THING...
YES?

I'M QUITE A JUGGLER!
I CAN PLAY THE 14TH HUNGARIAN RHAPSODY ON MY SKULL!
I'LL GET MY BAG-PIPES!
I'LL GET MY VENTRILOQUIST'S DUMMY!
AARGH!
END

Art: Rex Lindsey

Originally printed in BETTY & VERONICA SPECTACULAR #17, JANUARY 1996

Betty and Veronica in "TWIST OF FATE"

Story: Frank Doyle Art: Dan DeCarlo
Letters: Bill Yoshida Colors: Barry Grossman

Originally printed in BETTY & VERONICA SPECTACULAR #17, JANUARY 1996

HELP! SOMEBODY HELP ME! I THINK I BROKE SOMETHING!

HANG ONTO ME! I'LL GET YOU TO THE NURSE!
OOOW! THE PAIN! THE PAIN!

WELL, IF IT HURTS THAT MUCH, WE'D BETTER HAVE AN X-RAY!
IT HURTS THAT MUCH!

A LITTLE LATER...
NOTHING IS BROKEN, VERONICA! BUT IT IS QUITE SWOLLEN AND DISCOLORED!
AIEEEE! MY BEAUTIFUL LEG, SWOLLEN AND DISCOLORED! THAT'S WORSE THAN THE PAIN!

IT'S MERELY A STRAIN, NOT A SPRAIN, GIRL! THIS ACE BANDAGE WILL HELP, AND I'LL LEND YOU A CANE TO MAKE WALKING EASIER!

WALKING? YOU THINK I CAN WALK ON THIS TERRIBLY MANGLED FOOT?
WELL, TRY TO KEEP IT ELEVATED AS MUCH AS POSSIBLE! IT SHOULD BE BETTER IN A FEW DAYS!
2

STOCK ROOM
I HAVE AN IDEA, RON! I'LL BORROW ONE OF THOSE ADJUSTABLE CHAIRS THEY USE IN THE OFFICE!
AS LONG AS IT GETS ME OFF MY FEET!
THERE! NOW GET IN THERE AND LEAN BACK!
BETTY, YOU'RE A GENIUS!
GREAT! THAT KEEPS MY POOR, INJURED FOOT ELEVATED NICELY!
WATCH THAT CANE...
OOF!
OOPS! SORRY, JUGHEAD!
YOU OUGHTA BE CAREFUL WITH THAT CANE!
DON'T YOU HAVE ANY SYMPATHY FOR A POOR, UNFORTUNATE, SICK WOMAN?
HMPH! I SHOULD BE SO POOR AND UNFORTUNATE!
DRIVE ON, BETTY! THERE'S NO COMPASSION IN THAT TWIT!
3

WHAT DO THEY CARE ABOUT A LOVELY, TALENTED, YOUNG LADY IN EXCRUCIATING PAIN AND...

CRASH!

WHO ASKED THEM TO PUT THAT STUPID TROPHY CASE RIGHT WHERE I WAS WAVING MY CANE?

(SIGH) THE WORLD IS FULL OF UNTHINKING INGRATES!
EXACTLY! I'M GLAD YOU AGREE WITH ME!

WHOOPS!
H-HEY!!
CRAK!!

FOR HEAVEN'S SAKE, ARCHIE, MUST YOU BE SO CLUMSY? DIDN'T YOU SEE THAT I WAS GRIEVOUSLY INJURED?
4

YOU SAW THAT, BETTY! DIDN'T HE WALK RIGHT INTO...
WHACK!
NOW WHAT? DON'T TELL ME SHE'S HAD A RELAPSE?
NO! SHE'S ALL RIGHT!!
BUT DO YOU HAVE THREE MORE CANES?
DON'T TELL ME! INJURED ANKLES IS THE LATEST FAD?
NO!
WE NEED THEM TO DEFEND AGAINST RONNIE!
CLIP!
END

Story & Pencils: Dan Parent Inks: Rudy Lapick

Originally printed in BETTY & VERONICA SPECTACULAR #18, APRIL 1996

Story: Frank Doyle Pencils: Dan DeCarlo
Inks: Henry Scarpelli Letters: Bill Yoshida Colors: Barry Grossman

Originally printed in BETTY & VERONICA SPECTACULAR #18, APRIL 1996

THAT'S THE MONIKER, SIS, ON ACCOUNT OF I'M DEADLY DANGEROUS!
BRRR! YOU SCARE ME!

ER-- I SHOULD WARN YOU! YOU CAN'T WEAR THOSE BLADES IN THE HALLS!
SEZ WHO?

SAYS MR. WEATHERBEE, OUR PRINCIPAL!
OH! THE WARDEN, HUH?
R

LISSEN! LAST PLACE I WAS IN, WE RAN THINGS!
WE? WHO'S WE?

ME AN' THE BOYS! SEE YOU LATER!
?
!

(GASP) WHO'S THAT?
SOME NEW KID!
IF THE BEE SEES HIM HE WON'T GET TO BE AN OLD KID!
WOOSH!
RIVER
2

YIPE!
WATCH IT, MOMMA!!
HALT, WHOEVER YOU ARE!!
SCREEEEE

DOES THE WORD "DETENTION" MEAN ANYTHING TO YOU?
AH! MY HOME AWAY FROM HOME!

WE TRIED TO WARN YOU!
HEY! I WANTED DETENTION!

THAT'S WHERE I RECRUIT MOST OF MY BOYS!
YOUR "BOYS"?

YEAH! MY PACK! THE GUYS I HANG WITH!
THAT SORT OF THING IS FROWNED UPON IN OUR SCHOOL!

SIS, WHEN I GET ORGANIZED, I'LL BE CALLING THE SHOTS!
I THINK HIS BALLOON NEEDS A LITTLE DEFLATING!
3

LATER...
UH, OH! DO YOU SEE WHAT I SEE?
EEP! MIDGE! HE IS DEADLY AND DANGEROUS!

ER- MR. SNAKE! YOU LIKE THAT GIRL YOU WERE TALKING TO?
SHE'S GONNA BE SNAKE'S OL' LADY! THE BOSS ALWAYS GOT A OL' LADY!

D' YOU HEAR A HISSING SOUND?
COULD THAT BE HIS BALLOON LOSING AIR?
R

MR. SNAKE! EVERY "TAKE CHARGE" GUY NEEDS A RIGHT HAND MAN, RIGHT?
TRUE! YOU GOT SOMEONE IN MIND?

SNAKE! THIS IS MOOSE!
D-UH! YUH'RE WEARIN' BLADES IN SCHOOL! THAT'S A NO-NO!

DON'T WORRY, MOOSE! YOU WATCH MY BACK, I'LL HANDLE THE SMALL STUFF, SEE?
15
4

HEY! LONG AS YOU'RE ON MY TEAM, YOU GOTTA MEET MY OL' LADY!
D-UH! YUH BRANG YER MOM TO SCHOOL?

HA! NO, DUMMY! MY MAIN SQUEEZE! HERE SHE COMES NOW!

HIYA, BABY! SEE, MOOSE! THIS IS MY OL' LADY!
H-HELLO MOOSE!

I SEE ONE OF OUR NEW STUDENTS IS LEAVING ALREADY, GERALDINE! COULDN'T MEET OUR HIGH STANDARDS I GUESS!
RIGHT, CHIEF! TOO MUCH PRESSURE I SUPPOSE!

THEY'RE CARRYING HIM OUT, NOW!
?
END

Story: Dan Parent Pencils: Dan Parent & Dan DeCarlo
Inks: Henry Scarpelli Letters: Bill Yoshida Colors: Barry Grossman

Originally printed in BETTY & VERONICA SPECTACULAR #19, JULY 1996

HOW RIDICULOUS! THEY'RE HILARIOUS!
IT'S AMAZING WHAT PEOPLE WILL GO TO COURT OVER!
WELL, ARE YOU READY TO DO MY HAIR, BETTY?
CERTAINLY!
THIS BODY WAVE WILL LOOK GREAT!
I USUALLY PAY A FORTUNE FOR A HAIRSTYLE, BUT I PROMISED DADDY I WOULD ECONOMIZE!
NO PROBLEM! I DO MY OWN HAIR ALL THE TIME!
THIS BODY WAVE WILL LOOK GREAT ON YOUR HAIR!
WE'LL JUST SET THE TIME!
DING DONG!
OH, WHO COULD THAT BE? PLEASE GET IT, BETTY!
Vague
IT'S ARCHIE!
OH! I'M HIDING!
2

I DON'T WANT HIM TO SEE ME LIKE THIS!
I'LL GET RID OF HIM!

HI, ARCHIEKINS, I'M DOING RON'S HAIR! YOU'LL HAVE TO COME BACK LATER!
FIRST LET ME TELL YOU ABOUT... BLAH! BLAH!

45 MINUTES LATER...
OH, ARCHIE, YOU'RE SO SILLY! OH, NO! I FORGOT ABOUT RONNIE!
YOU'D BETTER GO!

FINALLY! IS IT TIME TO TAKE THIS OFF?
YEAH!
THIRTY MINUTES AGO!

I HATE TO LOOK!
IS IT ME?

WELL, YOU AND MAYBE LITTLE ORPHAN ANNIE!
EEEEEK!
3

HOW COULD YOU DO THIS TO ME ?!?
?

I'M SORRY! I GOT TIED UP WITH ARCHIE!
YOU DID THIS ON PURPOSE, SO I'D LOOK BAD TO ARCHIE!

HONEST, I DIDN'T! YOUR TIMER DIDN'T GO OFF! AND I WAS DISTRACTED BY ARCHIE!
YOU'VE GOT TO FIX THIS!

I'LL CALL THIS HOTLINE ON THE BOX!
HURRY!
Wilt

SOON...
WHAT'D THEY SAY?
TO GO TO A PROFESSIONAL!

IT'S SUNDAY NIGHT! I'LL HAVE TO SKIP SCHOOL AND DO IT TOMORROW!
NO WAY! NOT WITH YOUR GRADES, VERONICA!
4

BUT MY HAIR!
YOU CAN COVER IT UNTIL AFTER SCHOOL!

WAH!
THIS IS WAR, BETTY!
I FEEL TERRIBLE, RON!

SO...
HEY, IT'S QUEEN OF ANOTHER GALAXY!
HMPH! YOU DON'T KNOW FASHION, SIMPLETON!

WHAT'RE YOU HIDING, RICH GIRL?
HEY! LEAVE ME ALONE!

EEK!
YIKES! THAT IS SCARY!

I SHOULD SUE YOU, BETTY!
THIS WOULD BE GREAT FOR OUR LEGAL AFFAIRS CLASS THIS AFTERNOON!
5

WE'RE VIDEOTAPING MOCK COURT TRIALS FOR THE LOCAL TV STATION!
THIS ISN'T EVEN MOCK! IT'S FOR REAL!

SIGN ME UP! I WANT BLONDIE TO PAY FOR THIS HUMILIATION!
FINE! ANY COURT WOULD SEE YOU'RE JUST OVERREACTING ANYWAY!

SO...THE TRIAL BEGINS:
OKAY, CLASS, I'LL BE MONITORING FROM HERE!
WHO'S REPRESENTING YOUR CASES?

MY LAWYER IS FORSYTHE P. JONES!
REGINALD MANTLE IS MY ATTORNEY!

FINE! THE JUDGE MAY ENTER FROM HIS CHAMBERS NOW!

GAK! ARCHIE! WHO WOULD'VE THOUGHT!
WONDERFUL! THIS CASE IS AS GOOD AS WON!
TO BE CONTINUED 6

"HERE COMES THE JUDGE" PART II
THE CASE OF VERONICA LODGE VS. BETTY COOPER WILL NOW COME TO ORDER!
PROCEED WITH YOUR OPENING STATEMENTS!
JURY
IF YOU SAY HAMBURGER, FRENCH FRIES AND A LARGE DRINK, I'M GETTING ANOTHER LAWYER!

YOUR NOT-SO-HONORABLE HONOR, I INTEND...
HEY, WATCH THAT! I CAN HOLD YOU IN CONTEMPT!

WHY NOT? I'VE ALWAYS HELD YOU IN CONTEMPT!
GRRR!
KNOCK IT OFF, YOU TWO, AND GET WITH IT!
7

AS I WAS SAYING, I INTEND TO PROVE THAT BETTY COOPER DID WILLFULLY GIVE MY CLIENT THIS HIDEOUS HAIRDO!
SNIFF!

JUST LOOK AT IT! HOW CAN SHE SHOW HER FACE? SHE'S A FREAK! SHE LOOKS LIKE SHE FELL OFF THE CIRCUS TRAIN! SHE...
ENOUGH!!

I THINK YOU'VE GOTTEN YOUR POINT ACROSS!
I KNEW I SHOULD'VE TRIED TO GET THAT MATLOCK GUY TO HANDLE THIS!

YOUR HONOR, I INTEND TO PROVE MY CLIENT IS 100% NOT GUILTY!!
BUT I DID DO IT! IT WAS JUST AN ACCIDENT!

OKAY, SO SHE'S MORE LIKE 51%-ISH NOT GUILTY!
I'M DEAD!

PROSECUTION, YOU MAY CALL YOUR FIRST WITNESS!
YOUR... AHEM ... HONOR! I CALL VERONICA LODGE TO THE STAND!
8

MISS LODGE, CAN YOU TELL US WHAT HAPPENED ON THE NIGHT IN QUESTION?
I'LL (SOB) TRY!

SHE FORCED THE CHEAP HOME PERM ON MY HAIR AGAINST MY WILL! (SOB)
AND THEN LET ME WAIT WHILE SHE CONSORTED WITH THE JUDGE!
EEP!

IS THAT GIRL IN THIS COURTROOM, OR CAN YOU SEE, SINCE SHE PROBABLY GOT STUFF IN YOUR EYES?!
SHE'S RIGHT THERE!

LET THE RECORD SHOW THAT THE WITNESS POINTED TO ONE BETTY COOPER!
WHEW! WHAT A RELIEF! FOR A SECOND I THOUGHT SHE WAS POINTING TO ME!

LATER...
BETTY COOPER, BEFORE YOU ANSWER THE NEXT QUESTION, LET ME REMIND YOU YOU'VE SWORN TO TELL THE TRUTH!
YES!

HAVE YOU EVER FOUND YOURSELF ATTRACTED TO ME?
WHAT?!
9

AND THEN...
YOUR HONOR, I WOULD LIKE TO REQUEST A TEN-MINUTE RECESS BEFORE THE DEFENSE RE-CREATES THE EVENT!
JURY
HUH?

DON'T WORRY! I'LL DO IT RIGHT! WE'LL JUST EXPLAIN HOW THE ACCIDENT COULD'VE HAPPENED!
?
WILT HOME PERM

THE COURT WILL TAKE A TEN-MINUTE RECESS!
DUH...OH, GOODY! I HAVEN'T HAD RECESS SINCE GRADE SCHOOL!
JURY
15

EXCUSE ME, BUT I'VE GOT TO MAKE A PHONE CALL!
THAT'S OKAY! I SAW A FEW JURY MEMBERS I WANTED TO HIT ON!

TEN MINUTES LATER...
THIS COURT IS BACK IN SESSION!
DEFENSE, DO YOUR THING!
THANK YOU, YOUR HONOR!
JURY

MY CLIENT WAS SIMPLY APPLYING THE SOLUTION TO VERONICA'S HAIR LIKE SO WHEN THE DOORBELL RANG!
BUZZZ
HUH?!
10

IT'S A FIRE DRILL! EVERYONE LEAVE THE ROOM SINGLE FILE AND EXIT THE BUILDING!
BUZZ!
B-BUT...
I'M OUTTA HERE!

MR. WEATHERBEE, WHY DIDN'T YOU INFORM THE FACULTY WE WERE HAVING THIS?!
I ASKED HIM TO DO IT IMPROMPTU! KEEP THE KIDS OUT A WHILE LONGER WHILE WE CHECK THE SPRIN-KLER SYSTEM!

DADDY'S GENEROUS CONTRIBUTIONS TO THE FIREMEN'S RELIEF FUND SURE COME IN HANDY SOME-TIMES!
THAT PHONE CALL YOU MADE... YOU DIDN'T...

LATER...
THE COURT IS FINALLY BACK IN SESSION!
UH-OH!
MY HAIR! IT'S RUINED!!

WAH!
WE'LL SUE THE FIRE DEPARTMENT!
AN EYE FOR AN EYE, A BAD HAIRDO FOR A BAD HAIRDO!!
MS. GRUNDY, THIS ISN'T A TRIAL... IT'S A CIRCUS!
SIGH HAVE YOU CAUGHT ANY REAL-LIFE COURT CASES LATELY?!
THE END

Story: George Gladir Pencils: Dan DeCarlo
Inks: Mark Brewer Letters: Bill Yoshida Colors: Barry Grossman

Originally printed in BETTY & VERONICA SPECTACULAR #19, JULY 1996

I HAD THE FAMOUS MADAME CHAPEAU DESIGN THIS "POWER HAT" FOR ME!
WOW! VERONICA! IT'S GOT A A PHONE ...A CALCULATOR!
CEO
MEMO

NATURALLY! IT'S AN AUTHENTIC POWER HAT!
MEMO

MY DAD'S PAPER IS SENDING A PHOTO-GRAPHER THIS MORNING TO PHOTOGRAPH THE MOST INTERESTING GOOFY HAT!

SO IT'LL BE MY PHOTO THAT'LL BE IN THE PAPERS!
NOT NECESSARILY!

THIS PHOTOGRAPHER IS VERY SUPERSTITIOUS!
...HE'LL PROBABLY PICK BETTY'S HAT BECAUSE OF ALL ITS LUCKY SYMBOLS!

DRAT! HOW DO I MAKE HIM PICK ME?
HMM! I'VE AN IDEA!

BORROW BETTY'S HAT FOR THE FIRST PERIOD... THAT'S WHEN THE PHOTO-GRAPHERS WILL BE HERE!
...TELL BETTY YOU NEED HER LUCKY HAT FOR AN EXAM YOU'RE TAKING!
REGGIE, YOU'RE SO CLEVER!
2

SO YOU DON'T MIND IF WE SWITCH HATS FOR THE FIRST PERIOD?
I'D BE HAPPY TO... IF YOU THINK IT'LL BRING YOU LUCK!

RIVERDALE POST

THEY SWITCHED HATS! THERE'S BETTY IN RON'S POWER HAT!

YUK! YUK! I THINK I'LL PLAY A GAG AND CALL HER PHONE!
PHONE

RING!! RING!! RING!!
?!

BETTY! THAT RINGING SOUND IS COMING FROM YOUR HAT!
OH, DEAR!
3

I HAVE REPEATEDLY WARNED EVERYONE NOT TO BRING PHONES TO CLASS!
I WILL NOT TOLERATE THESE NOISY INTERRUPTIONS!

REPORT TO THE PRINCIPAL'S OFFICE RIGHT NOW!
GULP! YES, MISS GRUNDY!
A²+B²=C²
πR²

I'M SORRY I'M LATE FOR YOUR GOOFY HAT DAY!
NO PROBLEM!

SIR, MISS GRUNDY SENT ME TO SEE YOU! THE PHONE ON MY POWER HAT WENT OFF!
CEO

HA! HA! THAT'S THE FUNNIEST THING I'VE EVER HEARD OF!

THAT'S A GREAT STORY!
THERE'S NO MORE NEED FOR ME TO LOOK ANY FURTHER!
CLICK! CLICK! CLICK!
CEO
4

REGGIE, I DON'T SEE THAT PHOTOGRAPHER ANYWHERE AROUND!
WHAT HAPPENED?

WHO KNOWS?
MAYBE HE DIDN'T SHOW UP 'CAUSE THE NEWSPAPER DECIDED TO CANCEL THE STORY!

THE NEXT DAY...
WOW! MY DAD'S PAPER DID COVER GOOFY HAT DAY... WITH A WHOLE PAGE!
LET ME SEE! LET ME SEE!

OBVIOUSLY THE PHOTOGRAPHER MUST HAVE TAKEN MY PHOTO WHEN I WASN'T LOOKING!

AWK! IT'S A PICTURE OF BETTY... NOT ME!!
YOUR POWER HAT TURNED OUT TO BE A REAL LUCKY HAT!
SCENE
RIVERDALE HIGH HOLDS GOOFY HAT DAY
"POWER HAT" WINS BETTY COOPER A TRIP TO THE PRINCIPAL'S OFFICE WHEN PHONE RINGS.
CEO
WACKIEST HAT OF THEM A
END

Story: Dan Parent Pencils: Dan DeCarlo & Dan Parent
Inks: Mark Brewer Letters: Bill Yoshida Colors: Barry Grossman

Originally printed in BETTY & VERONICA SPECTACULAR #20, OCTOBER 1996

THE ONLY ROCKS I LIKE ARE THESE DIAMOND KIND!
SUIT YOURSELF!

WHAT IS THAT?
IT'S A MAN-MADE CLIMBING WALL! IT GETS YOU PREPARED FOR THE REAL THING!

WOW!
GO, BETTY!
SHE'S REALLY GOT A KNACK FOR IT!

HELLO! I'M VERONICA LODGE! YOU MUST BE PLEASED TO MEET ME!
ER - YEAH! THRILLED!

WELL! THEY'VE GIVEN ME THE COLD SHOULDER FOR GOLDILOCKS!
CAN WE JOIN YOU?

SURE!
ARE YOU GOING TO CLIMB NEXT MONTH'S CLIMBING EVENT AT McKINLEY PARK?
2

WELL, I'M NOT SURE!
AW, C'MON, YOU'LL BE GREAT!
YEAH, YOU'VE GOT TO!

WELL, IF YOU INSIST... OKAY!
YAY!!
ALL RIGHT!

HOW SICKENING!
I'LL SHOW THEM A THING OR TWO! ANYBODY CAN CLIMB A DUMB ROCK!

VERONICA! YOU'RE NOT READY FOR THIS YET!
MAKE WAY FOR GREATNESS!

VERONICA! AT LEAST PUT ON A BEGINNER'S HARNESS!
HARNESS SHMARNESS!

OH, DEAR! WHERE ARE ALL THE ROCKS TO STEP ON?
YOU DON'T STEP! YOU LOOK FOR SMALL FINGER-HOLDS AND TOE-HOLDS!
3

NOW YOU TELL...
WOW!
ME!!!

HA! WHAT A COMEDIAN!
ANOTHER LUCILLE BALL!

LATER...
VERONICA, DO YOU REALLY WANT TO LEARN ALL ABOUT CLIMBING?
YES! I'M VERY MOTIVATED!

AND MY MOTIVATIONS ARE THOSE TWO HUNKS AT THE GYM!
IT'S NOT JUST ABOUT CLIMBING!

WE'VE GOT TO WORK OUR WHOLE BODY! WE'VE GOT TO BE FIT EVERYWHERE!
YEAH, RIGHT! LET ME FINISH THIS BON BON!
POP'S

THE NEXT DAY...
VERONICA! ARE YOU EVER GOING TO WORK OUT WITH ME?
I AM! THIS NAIL PAINTING GIVES ME GREAT WRIST CONTROL!
4

PUFF! PUFF! WHY ARE WE DOING THIS AGAIN?
IT IMPROVES OUR CARDIOVASCULAR SYSTEM!

WE'LL NEED ALL THE STRENGTH WE CAN GET FOR OUR CLIMB, VERONICA!
VERONICA?

VERONICA! GET UP!!
CAN'T WE REST? WE'VE BEEN RUNNING FOR MILES!

MILES? WE'RE JUST BARELY OUT OF YOUR FRONT WALK!
YIKES?

SO...
WE'RE CLIMBING UP THAT HILL?!
FOR PRACTICE! COME ON!

OH NO! I TRIPPED ON MY SHOELACE!
SNAP
5

WAH!
OUT OF MY WAY, MR. SQUIRREL!
SHE'S HOPELESS!
?
HEY! HE'S GOT MY EARRING!
GIVE THAT BACK TO ME, YOU BEAST!
WOW! LOOK AT HER GO!
THAT IS REAL GOLD!
I GOT IT AT SAK'S FOURTH AVENUE, THROUGH A MASSIVE CROWD!
NOBODY TAKES MY JEWELRY AND LIVES TO TELL ABOUT IT!
THERE! I AM VICTORIOUS!
?
HMMM! SHE MIGHT NOT BE SO HOPELESS AFTER ALL!
TO BE CONTINUED
6

"CLIMB EVERY MOUNTAIN" PART II
OKAY, LET'S GET STARTED!
HI, BOYS! FANCY MEETING YOU HERE!
I CAN'T BELIEVE YOU'RE ATTEMPTING THIS!
I'VE IMPROVED A LOT SINCE YOU'VE SEEN ME LAST!
VERONICA! YOU'RE NOT GOING TO WEAR THAT OUTFIT, ARE YOU?
OF COURSE! I HAD IT ESPECIALLY DESIGNED FOR TODAY!
DON'T EMBARRASS ME, PLEASE!
7

YOU'LL BE PROUD OF ME, BETTY! SO WILL YOU, BOYS! LET'S GO!

BEFORE WE GO, YOU NEED TO WEAR THESE CLIMBING BOOTS!
BUT THESE LOVELY PUMPS WILL HELP ME GET A GRIP IN THOSE CREVICES!

ON! NOW!!!
SHEESH! HOW PUSHY!

SO...
I-I'M SCARED, BETTY!
VERONICA! YOU CAN'T BE!

YOU'RE ONLY THREE FEET OFF THE GROUND!
IT LOOKS SO MUCH FURTHER FROM HERE!

OKAY, I HATE TO DO THIS...
GIMME YOUR NECKLACE!
SNAP!
8

GIVE THAT BACK!
IF YOU WANT IT... COME AND GET IT!

WOW! LOOK AT VERONICA GO!
SHE HAS IMPROVED!
ZOOM!

WOW! SHE'S KEEPING UP WITH ME!
MINE!
MINE!
MINE!

LOOK! WE'VE MADE IT TO THE TOP!
GOOD! NOW GIVE ME MY NECKLACE!

SHALL WE GO BACK DOWN?
SURE, I... EEEEK!!

WE'RE WAY UP HERE?
WHAT'D YOU THINK, SILLY?
9

THERE'S NO WAY I'M CLIMBING DOWN THERE!
YOU HAVE NO CHOICE!

WANNA BET?
HELLO, SMITHERS! SEND THE HELICOPTER TO GET ME AT McKINLEY PARK!

WELL, THAT'S FINE FOR YOU! I'M CLIMBING DOWN!
SUIT YOURSELF, INDIANA JONES!

I'LL JUST HAVE A LITTLE PICNIC UNTIL THE HELICOPTER ARRIVES!

EEK! HELP!!
BETTY! IS THAT YOU?!

VERONICA! YOU'VE GOT TO HELP ME! MY HARNESS BROKE AND I CAN'T GET A GRIP!
OH, DEAR! WHAT DO I DO?
10

AH-HA! I'VE GOT IT!
I KNEW THESE WOULD COME IN HANDY!

HERE I COME TO SAVE YOU, DEAR FRIEND!
WOW! THESE HEELS DIG DEEP!
CRUNCH!

HOLD ON, BETTY!
I'M HOLDING! I'M HOLDING!

THERE! WE MADE IT! I KNEW THESE HEELS WOULD SUPPORT BOTH OF US!
VERONICA, YOU AND YOUR HEELS SAVED THE DAY!

OH, THE HELICOPTER'S HERE TO TAKE US TO SAFETY!
GUESS WHAT, SMITHERS? I SAVED BETTY'S LIFE!

LATER...
WOW! YOU REALLY SAVED BETTY FROM DANGER?
LIKE I'VE ALWAYS SAID... ALWAYS BRING A GOOD PAIR OF HEELS EVERY-WHERE YOU GO!
END

Story: Frank Doyle Art: Dan DeCarlo
Letters: Bill Yoshida Colors: Barry Grossman

Originally printed in BETTY & VERONICA SPECTACULAR #20, OCTOBER 1996

NOBODY DOESN'T KNOW VERONICA LODGE! I STAND OUT LIKE THE MOON IN A STARLESS SKY!

HI, BETTY! HOW GOES IT?
YOU'RE LOOKIN' GOOD, BETTY!

... AND ME? HOW ABOUT ME?

SEE? THEY JUST DIDN'T RECOGNIZE YOU, RON!

NO!
IT WAS A DELIBERATE SNUB! I OWE THOSE TWO... BIG TIME!

HI, BETS!
HI!

I WONDER WHO BETTY'S NEW FRIEND IS!
BEATS ME! I NEVER SAW HER BEFORE!
2

(GASP!) IT'S TRUE !! THE DISTINCTIVE ONE-IN-A-MILLION LOOK OF VERONICA LODGE IS A THING OF THE PAST!!

QUICK! IN HERE! A RESTORATION IS IN ORDER!
WANDA'S
WIG WAM

HMM! CLOSE, BUT NO CIGAR! IT'S JUST NOT ME!
IT'S CUTE THOUGH, RON!

CUTE DOESN'T CUT IT, DEARIE! RONNIE LODGE IS SPECTACULARLY BEAUTIFUL!

NOW THAT'S ME! I'LL TAKE IT!

HEY! THERE'S VERONICA NOW!
YOU PROMISED THAT WE COULD SWIM IN YOUR POOL TODAY!
YOU'RE RIGHT, KIDS! COME ON OVER!
3

WHEEE! THIS IS GREAT!
HEADS UP, CHARLEY!
THAT VERONICA LODGE IS THE GREATEST!
BEST IN THE WORLD!

NOW THAT'S MORE LIKE IT! THE OLD ADORATION IS BACK!
THEY DO SEEM TO LOVE YOU... AND YOUR POOL!!

MY! IT'S GETTING QUITE BREEZY! I WONDER IF WE'RE GOING TO GET RAIN!

C'MON, GANG! HOW ABOUT A SHOW OF APPRECIATION FOR OUR HOSTESS?

FOR SHE'S A JOLLY GOOD FELLOW, FOR SHE'S A JOLLY GOOD FELLOW- WHICH NOBODY CAN DENY!!!
4

WHOOPS! THAT WIND IS WHIPPING UP HARDER!

YIPE!
SOMEBODY CATCH THAT!!

HEY! THAT'S NOT VERONICA!!
SHE'S AN IMPOSTER!

WHAT'D YOU DO WITH OUR VERONICA, GIRLIE?
LET'S GET HER, GUYS!
NO! NO! I'M *ME*!!

(GLUB)
SECLUSION!! I'M GOING INTO SECLUSION UNTIL IT ALL GROWS BACK!
MEANWHILE, SHALL I DRY OUT THE OLD ADORATION?
The END

Story: Barbara Slate Pencils: Dan Parent
Inks: Jon D'Agostino Letters: Bill Yoshida Colors: Barry Grossman

Originally printed in BETTY & VERONICA SPECTACULAR #21, JANUARY 1997

Betty and Veronica in The BIG Trip! PART 1
MAYBE I CAN BE THE NEXT ALL-AMERICAN GIRL!
Sixteen
2

THE NEXT WEEK...

OMIGOSH! IT'S FROM SIXTEEN MAGAZINE!
16 MAGAZINE
Betty Cooper

WELL, THIS IS IT!
RIPPP!

I'M A FINALIST!!

WAIT 'TIL VERONICA HEARS ABOUT THIS!
3

RRING
WHO COULD BE CALLING SO EARLY?
YOUR BREAKFAST, MS. LODGE!

HELLO!
RON! IT'S ME, BETTY!

GUESS WHAT?! I'M A FINALIST IN THE ALL-AMERICAN GIRL CONTEST FOR SIXTEEN MAGAZINE!

THEY'RE FLYING ME TO NEW YORK CITY!
THAT'S GREAT, BETTY! I'M SO HAPPY FOR YOU!

BETTY COOPER! THE ALL-AMERICAN GIRL!
JEALOUS, ARE WE?
4

JEALOUS?! ME, VERONICA LODGE, ONLY THE MOST POPULAR GIRL IN ALL OF RIVERDALE HIGH, JEALOUS OF BETTY?
WHO ARE YOU ANYWAY?
I'M YOUR CONSCIENCE, VERONICA! SO TRY TO BE HONEST!
WELL, MAYBE A TEENSY BIT JEALOUS!
BUT BETTY IS MY BEST FRIEND!
AND SHE'D DO ANYTHING FOR YOU!
I KNOW! I'LL THROW HER A BIG PARTY TO SHOW JUST HOW GRACIOUS I CAN BE!
THAT-A-GIRL!
BESIDES, WITH BETTY OUT OF TOWN, I CAN HAVE ARCHIE ALL TO MYSELF!
5

THAT SATURDAY NIGHT...
CONGRATULATIONS
CONGRATULATIONS, BETTY!
DOES SIXTEEN MAGAZINE NEED A HANDSOME MALE MODEL?
DON'T FORGET ABOUT ALL OF US WHEN YOU BECOME A BIG STAR!
I'M PROUD OF BETTY, BUT IT WILL BE HER FIRST TIME AWAY FROM HOME!
DON'T WORRY, DEAR! KARA FROM SIXTEEN MAGAZINE WILL TAKE GOOD CARE OF OUR DAUGHTER!
THIS SURE IS A GREAT PARTY!
IT WAS SO GENEROUS OF YOU TO THROW BETTY THIS PARTY, VERONICA!
THAT'S JUST THE WAY I AM, ARCHIEKINS!

THANK YOU, EVERYBODY! YOU'RE THE BEST FRIENDS IN THE WHOLE WIDE WORLD!

AND THANK YOU, RONNIE! I'LL CALL YOU EVERY NIGHT FROM NEW YORK!
I CAN'T WAIT TO HEAR ABOUT EVERYTHING, BETTY!
HAVE A GREAT TRIP!
TO BE CONTINUED-6

THE BIG TRIP! PART 2

A LOT OF PHOTO OP!

BETTY COOPER ?
THAT'S ME!
KARA, FROM SIXTEEN, TOLD ME TO EXPECT YOU!

I HOPE YOU WILL FIND YOUR STAY AT STRUMP TOWER ENJOYABLE, MS. COOPER!
WOW! THIS ROOM IS PHAT!

WELCOME, BETTY! LOOK IN THE CLOSET FOR YOUR WARDROBE. BE IN THE LOBBY AT 6:00.
Kara

IT LOOKS LIKE VERONICA'S CLOSET!

GEE, I PROMISED TO CALL HER!

BUT I BETTER GET READY SO I CAN LOOK MY VERY BEST!
8

AT 6 O'CLOCK!
WELCOME TO NEW YORK! I'M KARA FROM SIXTEEN MAGAZINE!
HI, I'M ELAINA!
I'M KIM!
I'M BETTY!

CONGRATULATIONS TO ALL OF YOU FOR BEING CHOSEN BY SIXTEEN FOR THE "ALL-AMERICAN GIRL"!

AND NOW LET'S GET ROLLING FOR A NIGHT ON THE TOWN!

FIRST WE'LL DINE AT "RESTAURANT IN THE PARK" WHERE FAMED PHOTOGRAPHER SKOVOOLO WILL TAKE PICTURES AND THEN ON TO "IN" FOR DANCING AND MORE PHOTO OPPORTUNITIES!
9

WOW! A BLUE CHANDELIER!
LOOK THIS WAY, BETTY!

CLICK
CLICK
BEAUTIFUL, BETTY!
CLICK

AND SOON...
WHY ARE ALL THOSE PEOPLE WAITING IN LINE?

EVERYONE WANTS TO GET INTO "IN"!
IN

BUT DON'T WORRY, WE CAN GO RIGHT IN!
10

WOW! EVEN THE "HARVEST BALL" NEVER LOOKED LIKE THIS!
WANNA DANCE?
SURE!
HE'S SUCH A GREAT DANCER!
MUCH BETTER THAN ARCHIE!
11

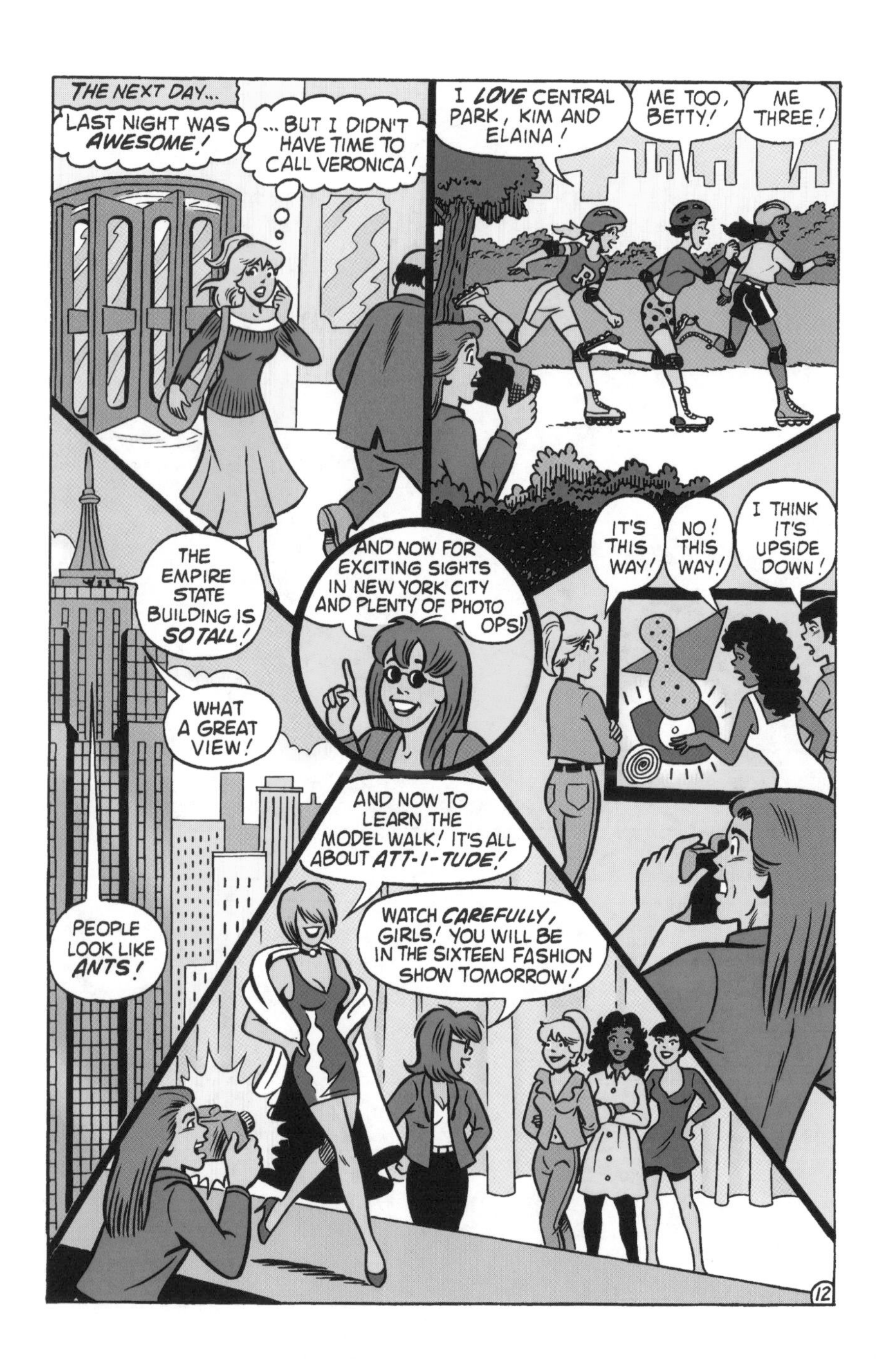
THE NEXT DAY...
LAST NIGHT WAS AWESOME!
...BUT I DIDN'T HAVE TIME TO CALL VERONICA!
I LOVE CENTRAL PARK, KIM AND ELAINA!
ME TOO, BETTY!
ME THREE!
AND NOW FOR EXCITING SIGHTS IN NEW YORK CITY AND PLENTY OF PHOTO OPS!
THE EMPIRE STATE BUILDING IS SO TALL!
WHAT A GREAT VIEW!
PEOPLE LOOK LIKE ANTS!
IT'S THIS WAY!
NO! THIS WAY!
I THINK IT'S UPSIDE DOWN!
AND NOW TO LEARN THE MODEL WALK! IT'S ALL ABOUT ATT-I-TUDE!
WATCH CAREFULLY, GIRLS! YOU WILL BE IN THE SIXTEEN FASHION SHOW TOMORROW!
12

GIRLS! GIRLS! GIRLS! I'VE GOT GREAT NEWS!

MONTEL MILLIONS WANTS YOU ON HIS SHOW!
WOW!

MONTEL MILLIONS IS MY FAVORITE TALK SHOW HOST!
ME?! BETTY COOPER! ON TV!

AND SO...
ARE YOU GIRLS HAVING FUN?
OH, YES!
I LOVE NEW YORK!
Montel

I'M HAVING THE BEST TIME OF MY LIFE!

OF COURSE, ONLY ONE OF YOU CAN BE THE SIXTEEN ALL-AMERICAN GIRL...
Montel
13

DO YOU FEEL COMPETITIVE?
NO!
NOT ME!
NEVER!
Montel

KIM AND ELAINA ARE MY BEST FRIENDS IN THE WHOLE WIDE WORLD!
SO WHO ARE WE?
AND I THREW HER A PARTY!
I NEVER THOUGHT BETTY COOPER COULD BE SO SHALLOW!
THERE GOES MY MODELING CAREER!
TO BE CONTINUED-14

THE BIG TRIP! PART 3

BEAUTIFUL!
SO WHOLE-SOME!
PLOP!
I'VE NEVER BEEN SO EMBARRASSED IN ALL MY LIFE!!
16

BACK AT STRUMP TOWER ...
NOW I'LL NEVER BE THE ALL-AMERICAN GIRL!

MORE LIKE THE FALL AMERICAN GIRL!

I FEEL LIKE SUCH A LOSER!

I NEED TO TALK TO MY BEST FRIEND!

RINGG!

LODGE RESIDENCE!
HELLO, IT'S BETTY! IS VERONICA THERE?
YES, SHE IS, MISS COOPER!
BETTY COOPER?!
17

TELL HER I MOVED!
!

OH, NO! NOW I'VE LOST THE CONTEST AND MY BEST FRIEND!

BACK AT RIVERDALE HIGH...
VERONICA! WAIT FOR ME!
WELL! IF IT ISN'T MISS BETTY COOPER GIVING ME THE HONOR OF HER PRESENCE!
18

I'M REALLY SORRY I HURT YOUR FEELINGS, VERONICA!

I GUESS I GOT SWEPT AWAY BY THE GLAMOUR OF NEW YORK AND FORGOT WHAT'S REALLY IMPORTANT...

YOU ARE MY REAL FRIENDS AT RIVERDALE HIGH!
CAN YOU EVER FORGIVE ME?
GOOD FRIENDS FORGIVE AND FORGET!

I ACCEPT YOUR APOLOGY, BETTY!
THANKS, RON! YOU'RE THE BEST FRIEND IN THE WHOLE WIDE WORLD!!
HI, GIRLS!
19

HI, ARCHIE! I HOPE YOU'RE NOT ANGRY WITH ME!
I'M JUST GLAD TO SEE THE GOOD OL' BETTY COOPER IS BACK!

ME, TOO! I'M SO HAPPY EVERY-THING IS BACK TO NORMAL!

BY THE WAY, I JUST GOT TWO TICKETS FOR THE HARVEST BALL!

WILL YOU GO WITH ME, VERONICA?
I'D LOVE TO ARCHIEKINS!

TOO NORMAL!
RIVERDALE HIGH
END

Story: Mike Pellowski **Pencils:** Mike Worley
Inks: Jon D'Agostino **Letters:** Bill Yoshida **Colors:** Barry Grossman

Originally printed in BETTY & VERONICA SPECTACULAR #21, JANUARY 1997

Art: Dan Parent

Originally printed in BETTY & VERONICA SPECTACULAR #22, MARCH 1997

Betty and Veronica in ISN'T IT Romantic?

Story & Pencils: Dan Parent

Inks: Rudy Lapick Letters: Bill Yoshida Colors: Barry Grossman

Originally printed in BETTY & VERONICA SPECTACULAR #22, MARCH 1997

GIGGLE THIS IS HILARIOUS! BETTY'S WRITING SOME SORT OF ROMANCE STORY!
I'LL PRINT IT OUT BEFORE SHE GETS BACK!

...THIS'LL MAKE FOR GOOD READING LATER!
OKAY, I'M READY!

A COUPLE OF WEEKS LATER...
VERONICA! GUESS WHAT?
YOU'RE FINALLY CHANGING YOUR LAME HAIRDO?

VERY FUNNY! HA! HA! NO! I'M BEING PUBLISHED!
HOW SO?

I WROTE A TEEN ROMANCE STORY! IT'S GOING TO BE IN "YOUNG LASS" MAGAZINE!
PART ONE IS IN NEXT MONTH'S ISSUE, TO BE FOLLOWED BY OTHER CHAPTERS LATER!

WELL, CONGRATULATIONS!
OH MY, IT'S LATE! GOTTA RUN!
2

WAH!! DADDY! BETTY'S AN AUTHOR AND I'M NOT!
OH, DEAR! WHAT'S WRONG NOW?

BETTY'S ROMANCE STORIES ARE GOING TO BE IN "YOUNG LASS"! I WANT TO BE PUBLISHED!
DON'T YOU OWN A TEEN MAGAZINE, DADDY?

YES! "SIXTEEN-AND-A-HALF"! BUT I'M NOT THE EDITOR! ONLY SHE CHOOSES CONTENT!
BUT YOU COULD PULL A FEW STRINGS, RIGHT?
I'LL TALK TO HER! THAT'S ALL!
THANK YOU, DADDYKINS!

SO...
VERONICA, A YOUNG ROMANCE SERIES DOES INTEREST ME!
BUT YOU'LL HAVE TO PROVE TO ME YOU'RE A GOOD WRITER FIRST!

SO...
OH, DEAR! I'M TOTALLY BLANK!
HMM! HERE'S BETTY'S STORY!
3

MAYBE I COULD BORROW A THING OR TWO FROM HER!

SO...
VERONICA! THIS STORY IS FABULOUS! I'M RUSHING IT INTO OUR NEXT ISSUE!
FANTASTIC! WAIT UNTIL I TELL ALL OF RIVERDALE!
MAYBE I SHOULD WAIT TO TELL BETTY!

RON! IS IT TRUE YOU GOT PUBLISHED IN THE RECENT "16½"?
ARCHIE JUST TOLD ME! LET'S FIND A COPY!
SPORT PARADE
SPY
LIVE
SEE!

OH, IT'LL JUST BORE YOU! LET'S GO TO THE MALL!
I'M READING IT-- I INSIST!
ON SALE
LOOK

SOON...
SO, WHAT DO YOU THINK?
I'LL TELL YOU WHAT I THINK!! YOU RIPPED ME OFF!

ALL YOU DID WAS CHANGE THE CHARACTERS' NAMES FROM TODD AND LITA TO ROD AND LIZA!
AND FROM "YOUNG HEARTS AFIRE" TO "YOUTHFUL HEARTS AFIRE"!
4

NO COURT WILL EVER CONVICT ME!
MINE HASN'T GONE TO PRESS YET! NOW I'LL HAVE TO EXPLAIN THIS TO MY EDITOR! IT'LL NEVER COME OUT NOW!

THANKS A LOT, FORMER FRIEND!
OH, YOU'LL GET OVER IT SOON ENOUGH!

A FEW WEEKS LATER...
VERONICA, YOUR STORY IS A BIG HIT!
THEY WANT TO INTERVIEW YOU ON TV'S "THE ROSIE O' LAKE" SHOW!

SHE'S GOING TO ASK YOU ABOUT THE NEXT CHAPTERS OF THE STORY!
BY THE WAY, I'LL NEED THE NEXT CHAPTER BY NEXT WEEK!

GULP! I THINK I'M IN OVER MY HEAD!
IF ONLY BETTY WAS STILL SPEAKING TO ME! MAYBE IF I BEG...

SOON...
YOU'LL WHAT? YOU'LL HELP ME? THANK YOU! THANK YOU!
LET'S JUST SAY I WANT THIS STORY TO WORK!

SO...
SO, WHAT WILL HAPPEN TO ROD AND LIZA ?
ER-UM-HERE'S A PREVIEW! ROD WILL GET ABDUCTED BY ALIENS, AND LIZA JOINS THE CIRCUS!
Rosie

HA! HA! YOU JOKER, YOU! WHAT REALLY HAPPENS?
ER-THAT'S REALLY IT!
Rosie

OH!
TIME FOR OUR NEXT GUEST...

SO...
VERONICA, THIS STORY IS LUDICROUS! DID YOU REALLY WRITE THAT FIRST CHAPTER?
WELL...

BETTY! YOU SET ME UP! YOU WROTE A RIDICULOUS FOLLOW-UP TO MAKE ME LOOK STUPID!
RON, YOU GOT YOURSELF INTO THIS MESS!

LUCKILY, YOUR EDITOR WILL BE PUBLISHING MY NEW WORK NOW, WITH ME GETTING THE CREDIT!
LIKE I SAID, I WANT THIS STORY TO WORK! IT LOOKS LIKE IT HAS!
END

Story: Barbara Slate Pencils: Dan Parent
Inks: Rudy Lapick Letters: Bill Yoshida Colors: Barry Grossman

Originally printed in BETTY & VERONICA SPECTACULAR #23, MAY 1997

WOW! HERE'S VA-VA-VANILLA!
VA VA Vanilla

IT SMELLS OUTRAGEOUS!
KNOCK! KNOCK!

BETTY COOPER! WHAT ARE YOU STILL DOING IN YOUR---

...ROOM?
SNIFF
SNIFF

SOMETHING SMELLS WON-DER-FUL!

MAR-VE-LOUS! 'TIS WON-DER-FUL!
2

MOM SINGING? SOMETHING VERY STRANGE IS GOING ON!

AND SOON...
IS IT MY IMAGINATION...

...OR IS THE ANIMAL AND BIRD WORLD PAYING A LOT OF ATTENTION TO ME?

THEY SEEM TO BE ATTRACTED TO MY PERFUME!

YO! BETTY!
HI, JUGHEAD! WHAT'S UP?
3

SNIFF
SNIFF

BETTY, BETTY, BETTY... WHEN I CALL YOUR NAME, I GET HEADY!
!

JUGHEAD RECITING POETRY?!

THIS PERFUME IS A MAJOR PHENOMENON!

LATER THAT AFTERNOON...
WHY ARE ALL THE BOYS FOLLOWING BETTY COOPER?
4

OBVIOUSLY, THEY HAVEN'T SEEN ME YET!

!
HI, VERONICA!

HEY, BETTY! WAIT UP!

SHE LOOKS THE SAME... SHE ACTS THE SAME...
SNIFF
SNIFF

WHAT'S THAT PERFUME YOU'RE WEARING, GIRLFRIEND?
UH-OH! SHOULD I TELL HER?
5

OF COURSE YOU SHOULD! SHE'S YOUR BEST FRIEND!
ARE YOU CRAZY? SHE'LL BUY IT AND THEN YOU CAN KISS ALL THIS ATTENTION GOODBYE!
POOF
POOF!

I KNOW! LET'S MAKE A DEAL!
WHAT IS THIS? A QUIZ SHOW?

NO! IT'S A PARTNERSHIP!
I TELL YOU MY SECRET FORMULA...

AND YOU BUY THE PRODUCT!
THEN WE SHARE THE PERFUME 50/50!

IT'S A DEAL!
CONTINUED-
6

Betty and Veronica in Scents of Humor PART 2
JUST MIX A LITTLE RUBY RED, ADD A SPLASH OF VA-VA-VANILLA...

AND VOILA! THE SECRET FORMULA!

NOW THAT I WILL BE WEARING THIS PERFUME, ALL THE BOYS WILL BE AFTER ME ... AGAIN!
7

STILL... BETTY HAS BEEN GETTING A LOT OF ATTENTION LATELY!

AND EVEN THOUGH MY ARCHIEKINS ONLY HAS EYES FOR ME...

SOMETIMES HIS NOSE GETS CONFUSED!
BUG SPRAY

PERHAPS I SHOULD ADD AN EXTRA INGREDIENT TO BETTY'S PERFUME!
BUG SPRAY
TOXZE

LATER THAT DAY...
NOW THAT RONNIE HAS MY SECRET FORMULA, ALL THE BOYS ARE IGNORING ME!
8

WHAT'D I TELL YOU?
DON'T SAY I DIDN'T WARN YOU!

YOU KEEP LISTENING TO THAT AWFUL ANGEL, YOU'LL END UP BEING THE BRIDESMAID BUT NEVER THE BRIDE!

COULD THAT BE TRUE?
LET'S GET THIS PARTY SWINGIN'! I GOT THE NEW PUMPKIN BUMPKIN CD!

LET'S DANCE, RON!
SURE, ARCH!

I'M NEXT, RONNIE!
THEN, ME!

WHY ARE ALL THESE MOSQUITOES PICKING ON ME?
I GUESS THEY LOVE YOUR PERFUME, TOO, RONNIE!
9

AHHHHHH!!!!!

I CAN'T STAND IT! I'M GOING HOME!

GEE, I WONDER WHY THOSE MOSQUITOES WEREN'T BITING ME, TOO!

I'M WEARING THE SAME PERFUME AS VERONICA!
SNIFF! SNIFF!

I SMELL SOME FOUL PLAY!
HMMMM ...

DO YOU WANT TO DANCE, BETTY?
SURE, ARCH!
HAVE FUN!
10

LATER THAT NIGHT...
THAT WAS A FAB PARTY, ARCHIE!
IT WAS AWESOME, BETTY! I JUST HOPE RONNIE'S FEELING OKAY!
SHE GOT SOME AWFUL BUG BITES!
BETTY AND MY ARCHIE TOGETHER!!

I HATE THIS PUTRID PERFUME!

PLOP!
GREAT CATCH, BETTY!
THANKS, ARCH!

BUT WHY WOULD RONNIE THROW HER PERFUME OUT THE WINDOW?
I GUESS SHE LOST HER SCENTS OF HUMOR!
The END

Story & Pencils: Dan Parent

Inks: Rudy Lapick Letters: Bill Yoshida Colors: Barry Grossman

Originally printed in BETTY & VERONICA SPECTACULAR #23, MAY 1997

GET A LOAD OF THIS KOOKY ALIEN COSTUME!
I'VE GOT TO TRY IT ON!

HOW DO I LOOK?
OUT OF THIS WORLD!

BUT IT'S NOT VERY SLIMMING!!
I'VE GOT TO GET IT OFF!

GRUNT! THIS ZIPPER'S STUCK! CAN YOU HELP ME?
OKAY, HOLD ON!

MAN, THIS THING IS STUCK!
I'LL GET SOME SCISSORS AND CUT YOU OUT!

DON'T YOU DARE! WE CAN'T RUIN THESE EXPENSIVE COSTUMES!
BUT I'VE GOT TO GET HOME FOR MY 3:30 MANICURE!
2

HOW ABOUT THIS! I'LL COME HOME WITH YOU AND WE'LL GET SOMEONE THERE TO HELP ME?
SOUNDS GOOD! COME ON!

THIS COSTUME IS SO BIG I CAN BARELY FIT IN HERE!
WELL, I'M NOT PUTTING THE TOP DOWN, SO YOU'LL HAVE TO MAKE DO!

THEN I'LL HAVE TO CRUNCH LIKE THIS!
MY, HOW ROMANTIC!

SOON...
WHAT'S GOING ON IN THAT CAR, HAROLD?
MIND YOUR BUSINESS, MABEL!

EEK! OHMIGOSH! IT'S AN ALIEN ATTACK!
THANK GOODNESS I'VE GOT MY VIDEO CAMERA ON ME!

THIS OUGHT TO BE WORTH A FORTUNE TO OUR LOCAL NEWS!
3

WILL YOU LOOK AT THIS TAPE? I'VE SPOTTED AN ALIEN ABDUCTION!
LET'S SEE IT!
W·RIV TV 8

I DON'T KNOW! IT COULD BE A LOT OF THINGS!
HEY! THIS IS SWEEPS MONTH! RUN IT!

JUST RUN A TINY DISCLAIMER UNDER IT TO COVER OURSELVES!
YOU GOT IT!

MAN! THIS TRAFFIC IS TERRIBLE!
I KNOW! I CAN HEAR ALL THE TRAFFIC HELICOPTERS!
NEWS 2

WAIT! THOSE ARE NEWSCOPTERS! THEY'RE FILMING US FOR TV!
I'VE GOT A PORTABLE TV IN MY PURSE! I'VE GOT TO CHECK THIS OUT!
NEWS 3
CHOPPER

WE'RE ALL OVER THE TUBE! THEY THINK YOU'RE AN ALIEN AND I'M YOUR VICTIM!
GIRL ABDUCTED BY ET
4

THAT'S RIDICULOUS! THIS COSTUME IS SO FAKE LOOKING!
THAT NEVER STOPPED "LOST IN SPACE"!

OH DEAR, WE'VE GOT TO STOP AT THIS RED LIGHT!
HERE COMES A REPORTER!

MISS LODGE! DO YOU HAVE A COMMENT?
YES! HELP! HELP!
4

RON! ARE YOU TRYING TO ENCOURAGE THEM?
GIGGLE! I'M JUST HAVING A LITTLE FUN!

AND AS THE GIRL DROVE, THE ALIEN CROUCHED AROUND HER IN A THREATENING MANNER!
OUR BABY!!
THE ALIENS ARE COMING!

DON'T WORRY! THE POLICE ARE STAKED OUT FOR THEIR ARRIVAL!
DO YOU REALLY THINK IT'S AN ALIEN?
5

IT'S PROBABLY SOME THUG IN A COSTUME!
OH, LOOK! THEY'RE HERE!

VERONICA! I'VE GOT THE ZIPPER UNSTUCK!
GOOD! DON'T TAKE THE COSTUME OFF YET! HERE'S WHAT WE DO...

OKAY, YOU BAD ALIEN! SHOW YOUR TRUE COLORS!
OKAY, HERE GOES!

BE CAREFUL! HE MIGHT ZAP YOU!
WHAT'S SHE GOING TO DO?
ZIP!!

HI, EVERYBODY!
IT'S BETTY!
WAS SHE INSIDE THE ALIEN'S BODY?
IT'S A COSTUME, NITWIT!

LOOK! THE ALIEN SHED ITS SKIN AND LET THE EARTH GIRL LOOSE!
SOME PEOPLE JUST DON'T GET IT!
END

Betty and Veronica in Color Me Ron!

Story & Pencils: Dan Parent

Inks: Rudy Lapick Letters: Bill Yoshida Colors: Barry Grossman

Originally printed in BETTY & VERONICA SPECTACULAR #23, MAY 1997

I WILL! I'LL SHOW YOU!
I KNOW WHO MUST KNOW SOMETHING ABOUT THIS...

YOU WANT ME TO PAINT YOUR ROOM? SURE, I'LL HELP!
BUT IT MUST BE A VERY SPECIFIC COLOR!

I WANT YOU TO MATCH THE COLOR OF MY FAVORITE NAIL POLISH!
FINE! BRING IT WITH US TO THE PAINT STORE!

THEY'LL CUSTOM MIX THE COLOR FOR US!
THEY CAN DO THAT?

WOW! YOU'VE GOT A LOT TO LEARN, RON!
YEAH, WHATEVER!

CAN YOU MATCH THIS COLOR?
I'LL TRY!
AL'S PAINTS
2

SO...
COOL! LET'S PAINT!
YOU CAN START! I'LL JOIN YOU IN A MINUTE!

3 HOURS LATER...
WHAT DO I DO?
WELL, NOW THAT I'M ALMOST DONE, WE CAN CLEAN UP!

IT LOOKS FABULOUS!
C'MON! I'LL TAKE YOU TO LUNCH!

AFTER LUNCH...
EEK! IT'S LIGHTER THAN IT WAS BEFORE!
PAINT DRIES A BIT LIGHTER THAN WHEN APPLIED, RON...

BUT IT DOESN'T MATCH MY NAIL POLISH COLOR ANYMORE!
RON! IT'S EXTREMELY CLOSE!

I WANT IT EXACT! WE'VE GOT TO DO IT OVER!
OH, BROTHER!
3

SO...
YOU MUST MIX THIS PAINT SO IT MATCHES THIS COLOR WHEN IT'S DRY!
YES, YOUR MAJESTY!
AL'S PAIN

I TESTED IT ON THIS PAPER! IT'S BEEN BLOWN DRY...
AND IT MATCHES PERFECTLY!

SO...
RON! WE'RE OUT OF PAINT! YOU LAID IT ON TOO THICK!
OH DEAR, WE'D BETTER GET MORE!

THE STORE IS CLOSED! WE'LL GET MORE PAINT TOMORROW! G'NIGHT!
BUT IT'S SUCH A SMALL AREA!

I KNOW HOW TO FINISH THIS WITH WHAT I'VE ALREADY GOT!
BETTY WILL BE SO IMPRESSED WITH ME!

THE NEXT DAY...
WAH!! YOU CAN SEE WHERE I STARTED TO PAINT AGAIN! THE COLORS DON'T MATCH!
THAT'S WHAT YOU GET FOR PUTTING ACTUAL NAIL POLISH ON THE WALL!
4

I THOUGHT THE ACTUAL NAIL POLISH WOULD *WORK!*
I'VE GOT TONS OF PAINT FROM THE PAINT STORE!
WE'LL NEVER *RUN* OUT NOW!

I'M BEAT! I WAS UP HALF THE NIGHT!
I'LL DO THIS *FASTER* WITHOUT YOU! WHY DON'T YOU LEAVE ME *ALONE* FOR A WHILE?

OKAY! I'LL BE BACK! I'LL *SHOP* A *LITTLE!*
BUT NOT TOO *SOON!* PLEASE!

LATER...
HI, RON! YOUR ROOM IS DONE! BEAUTIFUL ISN'T IT? YOU'RE GONNA OWE ME BIG TIME!
WAH!!

WHAT'S WRONG? IT MATCHES *PERFECTLY!*
WE HAVE TO *REPAINT* IT!

MY FAVORITE NAIL POLISH IS BEING *DISCONTINUED!!*
PLOP!!
END

Story & Pencils: Dan Parent

Inks: Rudy Lapick Letters: Bill Yoshida Colors: Barry Grossman

Originally printed in BETTY & VERONICA SPECTACULAR #25, SEPTEMBER 1997

"JUST FOLLOW THE DIRECTIONS AND REWARDS WILL BE BESTOWED UPON YOU!"

HA! RON MUST BE MESSING WITH MY HEAD! YOU WOULD THINK SHE COULD DO SOMETHING MORE IMAGINATIVE!
BETTY

HI, BETTY!
HI, RON! WHAT'S UP WITH THIS "TREASURE HUNT" STUNT, ANYWAY?

YOU GOT ONE, TOO? I FOUND THIS ON MY FRONT DOORSTEP THIS MORNING!
YOU MEAN, YOU DIDN'T SEND THIS TO ME?

NO! IN FACT, I THOUGHT MAYBE THIS WAS SOMETHING YOU WERE UP TO!
IT'S NOT ME!

IT'S PROBABLY ONE OF THE GANG!
2

RIGHT! WE GO ON THIS ELABORATE SEARCH AND THERE'S ARCHIE WAITING FOR US!
CLAIMING HE'S OUR BIG TREASURE!

OR BETTER YET, I CAN REALLY SEE REGGIE DOING SOMETHING LIKE THAT!

BUT IT SAYS "REWARDS" WILL BE BESTOWED UPON US!
LIKE I NEED MONEY?

SO...
SORRY, GIRLS! I DIDN'T SEND THE NOTE!
NEITHER DID I!

SHOULD WE GO ALONG WITH THIS?
IT IS QUITE INTRIGUING!

LOOK! IT'S SOMETHING FOR US! OPEN IT!
Betty & Veronica
3

IT'S AN OFFICIAL TREASURE MAP! COOL!
Ye Olde Treasure Map

LET'S FOLLOW THE DIRECTIONS!
I'VE GOT AN IDEA!

IF WE'RE LOOKING FOR MONEY OR VALUABLES, ONE PERSON CAN HELP US OUT!
YOU MEAN SNIFF AROUND A BIT, EH?

RIGHT! THE PERSON WHO CAN HELP US IF WE GET LOST! THE GIRL WITH THE NOSE FOR MOOLAH...

LATER
CRICKET O' DELL!
THANKS FOR CALLING ME, GIRLS!

A TREASURE HUNT! WHAT A DREAM COME TRUE!
IN FACT, I'M PICKING SOME-THING UP!
4

I'M GETTING **WOOZY!** I **DETECT** FILTHY RICHNESS NEARBY!
MY NOSE LEADS ME...

...RIGHT TO VERONICA!
THANKS, GENIUS!

YOU'D BETTER DISCARD ALL YOUR MONEY SO IT DOESN'T THROW ME OFF!
AND TAKE A **BATH!** YOU MUST REMOVE ALL MONEY SCENT SO I DON'T GET **CONFUSED!**

IT'S TOO **LATE** FOR THAT!
WE RISE EARLY! TOMORROW OUR ADVENTURE BEGINS!

SO...
HERE WE GO! WE START AT THE "L"-SHAPED ROCK!
IT LOOKS LIKE OUR FIRST DESTINATION IS THIS LITTLE HILL!

HMM! THAT SEEMS EASY ENOUGH!
C'MON! LET'S GO!
5

LOOK! IS THAT IT OUT THERE?
IT MUST BE! IT'S MARKED WITH A RED FLAG!

COOL! LET'S GO!
MAYBE WE'LL GET SOME CLUES OR SOMETHING!

IS THERE ANYTHING HERE?
I'M GETTING THIS SINKING FEELING!

MAYBE THAT'S BECAUSE WE'RE SINKING!
EEK!

IT'S QUICKSAND! WE'RE DOOMED!
IT'S NOT QUICKSAND, BUT SOME KIND OF SINKHOLE!

THIS WAS SET TO MESS US UP!
IT'S A BOOBY TRAP!!
6

Betty and Veronica
in Treasure Quest!
PART TWO
PTOOEY!! I THINK I SWALLOWED A GALLON OF SAND!
BUT AT LEAST WE MADE IT OUT OF THERE!
AND WE HAVE ANOTHER CLUE!

"GO TO THE REEF PAST SMUGGLER'S POINT!"
C'MON! LET'S GO!

I DON'T SEE A CLUE!!
HERE'S A BOX! THIS MUST BE...
7

IT!...
EEK!!!
KA-BLAM!
A PAINT BOMB!
SOMEBODY WANTS US TO LOOK STUPID!
HERE'S ANOTHER CLUE! BRING THIS PACKAGE UP TO HUNT'S LANDING!
REFRESH
SOUNDS SIMPLE, BUT LET'S BE CAREFUL!
I DON'T NEED THIS ABUSE!
DO WE JUST WAIT HERE?
EEK! A SEAGULL IS AFTER THIS PACKAGE!
EEK! TONS OF SEAGULLS!
NO WONDER! THERE'S RAW FISH IN THERE!!
LOOK! THIS BIRD HAS A MESSAGE! LET ME SEE WHAT IT SAYS!
8

GO DOWN TO PIER 14! IF YOU CAN!
WHAT'S THAT ON MY HEAD? IT'S ALL YUCKY!!

YOU DON'T WANT TO KNOW, RON!
BUT YOU CAN GUESS WHAT A BUNCH OF SEA-GULLS CAN DO!
GRRRR!

SO...
OKAY! WE'RE HERE! NOW WHAT?
C-R-R-R-E-A-K!
DO YOU HEAR THAT? WE SHOULD KNOW BETTER...

SPLASH!!
WE DESERVE THIS!

HERE'S OUR CLUE!
"YOUR REWARD WILL BE AT THE CAVE ON THE SOUTH SIDE!"
CLUE

THIS BETTER BE THE END OF ALL THIS!
CRICKET, USE YOUR SNIFFER! IF WE DON'T SMELL ANYTHING, WE'LL GIVE UP THIS FARCE!
9

I SMELL SOMETHING! THIS IS ON THE LEVEL!
THERE'S A SHOVEL! DIG!
A TREASURE CHEST! WE'VE FOUND IT!
OPEN IT UP! OPEN IT UP!

WHAT IS IT?
IT'S A CAMERA! AND A MONITOR! WHAT'S GOING ON?

SURPRISE! YOU'RE ON CHERYL'S CAMERA! SMILE!!
CHERYL BLOSSOM! WE SHOULD'VE KNOWN!

WE'VE GATHERED TO SEE YOU RIVERDALE GOOBERS IN ACTION!!
BUT I KEEP MY PROMISES! YOUR REWARD IS IN THERE!

LOOK! GOLD COINS!
TOO BAD THEY'RE CHOCOLATE INSIDE!
WHAT A SCAM!!
10

HA! YOU ALL LOOK INSANE!
I THOUGHT YOU SMELLED MONEY!
I STILL DO! KEEP DIGGING!

THIS IS TOO MUCH! THE HUMAN BLOODHOUND KEEPS DIGGING FOR MORE!
CLUNK! WHAT'S THIS?

IT LOOKS LIKE ANIMAL BONES!
IT'S NOT JUST ANY ANIMAL...

IT'S A DINOSAUR!
OH MY GOODNESS!
THIS IS BEYOND VALUABLE! WAIT UNTIL MUSEUMS FIND THIS OUT!

WE'LL BE RICH FROM THIS FIND!
AND I'LL BE EVEN RICHER!
CHERYL! WHAT'S SO FUNNY ABOUT THIS?
ER... UM... ER...
YIPES!
END

Art: Dan Parent

Originally printed in BETTY & VERONICA SPECTACULAR #25, SEPTEMBER 1997

Story & Pencils: Dan Parent

Inks: Rudy Lapick Letters: Bill Yoshida Colors: Barry Grossman

Originally printed in BETTY & VERONICA SPECTACULAR #25, SEPTEMBER 1997

RON, YOU DON'T PURCHASE ONE, YOU JUST VOLUNTEER SOME TIME TO SPEND WITH ONE OF THESE GIRLS!

HMM ... SOUNDS EASY! LET'S GO GET ME ONE!
SHE MAKES THIS SOUND LIKE SHE'S BUYING A SCARF!

SO...
THIS IS JEANNIE, YOUR NEW LITTLE SISTER!
HI, JEANNIE! DO YOU WANT TO GO TO THE BEACH?
LITTLE SI
INC.

SURE!
FIRST, LET'S STOP AND BUY YOU SOME NEW BEACH CLOTHES AT LACEY'S!

ER- I DON'T HAVE ANY MONEY!
NO PROBLEM! I'M GOING TO TREAT MY NEW LITTLE SISTER!

WE'LL GO ON WITHOUT YOU!
SEE YOU LATER, GIRLS!
2

LATER...
MY GOODNESS! YOU BOUGHT ALL THAT FOR THE BEACH?
YES! AND THERE'S MORE IN THE CAR!

RON! DON'T GO OVERBOARD!
I CAN'T HELP IT! I'VE NEVER HAD A SISTER BEFORE!

C'MON, RHONDA! LET'S FINISH OUR DELUXE SAND CASTLE!
LET'S HELP THEM!

OH, NO! THAT'S COMMONER'S WORK! YOU'RE A LODGE NOW! WELL, SORT OF!
LET'S BASK IN THE SUN! BUT WEAR THIS HAT! WE CAN'T AFFORD WRINKLES!

THAT POOR KID! VERONICA'S SMOTHERING HER!
I CAN'T SEE ANYTHING!

OH LOOK, THERE'S TOM SUMMERS!
I HAVE A CRUSH ON HIM! I'M GOING TO SAY HI!
3

LISTEN, GIRLFRIEND! YOU'VE GOT TO PLAY HARD TO GET! WALK BY HIM IN AN ALOOF AND SOPHISTICATED WAY!
BUT I'M ONLY 12 YEARS OLD!
THEN IT'S TIME TO LEARN!
I'LL COACH YOU FROM OVER HERE!
HI, JEANNIE! NICE DAY, ISN'T IT?
HEY! CAN'T YOU HEAR ME?
THAT'S IT! JUST IGNORE HIM AND PLAY HARD TO GET!
FINE! I'LL GO TALK TO CINDY JENKINS!
THANKS A LOT, VERONICA! THIS BACKFIRED BIG TIME!
ER- I'M SORT OF OUT OF PRACTICE WITH 12-YEAR-OLDS!
C'MON! LET'S PAINT OUR NAILS!
4

BUT I WANT TO HAVE SOME FUN!
THEN I'LL LET YOU BRAID MY HAIR!

SOON...
RON'S ASLEEP! C'MON, JEANNIE! GO HAVE SOME FUN!
THANKS, BETTY!
ZZZ

SOON...
YAWN! WHERE'S JEANNIE? IT'S TIME TO ACCESSORIZE MY TRAVEL BAG!
I SENT HER OFF TO HAVE REAL FUN!

WHAT? HOW DARE YOU INTERFERE!
NOW WHERE IS SHE? JEANNIE? JEANNIE?

HMPH! I CAN'T FIND HER ANYWHERE!
THANKS FOR BUILDING THIS CASTLE!
TRUST ME, I KNEW IT WOULD COME IN HANDY!
END

Story & Pencils: Dan Parent

Inks: Rudy Lapick Letters: Bill Yoshida Colors: Barry Grossman

Originally printed in BETTY & VERONICA SPECTACULAR #25, SEPTEMBER 1997

GO ON!
HONESTLY! THEY'RE SUCH SIMPLE CREATURES!!

I'VE HEARD ENOUGH ABOUT HERCULES AND ZEENA!
YOU SAID IT...
ZZZ

ARCHULES! HOW IS MY BIG HUNK TODAY?
FINE, BETEENA! WHAT ARE YOU UP TO TODAY?

NOT MUCH! JUST MOVING A FEW BOULDERS AROUND!
COULD YOU MOVE OUT OF MY WAY, JUGHORSE?

SORRY! I'M JUST GRAZING A BIT!!
SWOOSH!

WHAT WAS THAT?
IT IS I, VEREENA, WARRIOR PRINCESS!
2

WHAT? I'M THE WARRIOR PRINCESS OF THIS BEACH!
GIRLS! GIRLS! CAN'T WE HAVE TWO WARRIOR PRINCESSES?
OH, COME NOW! THERE'S ONLY ONE WARRIOR PRINCESS PER BEACH!
YEAH! DON'T YOU KNOW THE RULES?
LET'S SETTLE THIS WITH A LITTLE ONE-ON-ONE COMBAT!
PUT UP YOUR DUKES!
HI-YA!
TAKE THIS!
PUT DOWN THAT SPEAR! SOMEONE COULD GET HURT!
KICK!!
OOF!!
HI-YA!
3

PREPARE TO BE ANNIHILATED, VERENA!
DREAM ON, BLONDIE!

WOMP!!
OH, NO! HELP!!

WAH!! YOU'VE DONE IT NOW! YOU'VE REALLY DONE IT!!
DID I BREAK ANYTHING?

YES! YOU BROKE MY NAIL!
DO YOU KNOW HOW HARD IT IS TO FIND A GOOD MANICURIST IN THESE ANCIENT TIMES?

OH, BROTHER!
THERE! THERE! VEREENA! LET ME CONSOLE YOU!

NO, LET ME!!
WE'LL NURSE YOU BACK TO HEALTH!
4

HEY! I'M SUPPOSED TO BE THE WINNER HERE!
I'M SUPPOSED TO BE THE WINNER!

BETTY, WAKE UP! YOU'RE HAVING A DREAM!!
H-HUH? OH, THANKS, VEREENA

VEREENA? WAKE UP, GIRL!
OUCH! OH, DARN, I BROKE A NAIL!

DON'T THINK THAT YOU CAN USE THAT JUST TO BECOME WARRIOR PRINCESS OF THIS BEACH!! DO YOU HEAR ME!!

ER- BETTY, I THINK EVERYONE HEARD YOU!
OOPS!
End

Story: Barbara Slate Pencils: Dan Parent
Inks: Jon D'Agostino Letters: Bill Yoshida Colors: Barry Grossman

Originally printed in BETTY & VERONICA SPECTACULAR #26, NOVEMBER 1997

SNIP!!!
FABULOUS!!
YEAH, BETTY!
CLAP! CLAP!

IF I HEAR ONE MORE TIME HOW GREAT BETTY IS, I THINK I'LL ...
HEY, RONNIE!

ISN'T BETTY BRILLIANT?
AHHHHH!
STUFF

WHAT'D I SAY, MOOSE?
I DUNNO, MIDGE!
SLAM!
DANCE
2

I'VE GOT TO THINK OF SOMETHING TO GET THE ATTENTION AWAY FROM BETTY!

I GOT IT! I'LL MAKE THE GRANDEST OF ALL GRAND ENTRANCES!

ALL EYES WILL BE UPON ME AS I GRACEFULLY STEP INTO THE ROOM...
HOW CAN I COMPETE?
SHE'S MAGNIFICENT!
WOW!

POOR BETTY COOPER...

SHE'LL JUST BE A FADED MEMORY...
3

BACK TO.....
HMMM... WE NEED A FEW MORE BALLOONS OVER THERE AND...

A-A-AH...

CHOOO!
OH NO!
YOU CAN'T BE GETTING SICK!

YOU'VE BEEN WORKING TOO HARD, BETTY!
WE CAN FINISH DECORATING WITHOUT YOU!
YOU'D BETTER GO HOME AND CHILL OUT!
DANCE
4

AND SOON...
I'M SORRY, SWEETHEART, BUT YOU'RE NOT GOING ANYWHERE TONIGHT!
YOUR TEMPERATURE IS 102°!
SNIFFLE SNIFFLE

I'M TOO SICK TO PARTY, MIDGE!
I'M SOOOO SORRY, BETTY!
ATTENTION, EVERYONE! BETTY COOPER IS SICK! SHE CAN'T COME TONIGHT!
THAT'S TERRIBLE!
OH, NO!

BUT BETTY PUT SO MUCH TIME AND LOVE INTO THIS EVENT!
IT WON'T BE ANY FUN WITHOUT HER!
I THINK I'VE GOT A WAY TO SAVE IT!
CONTINUED- 5

Betty and Veronica in
"GRAND Entrance"
PART 2
LET'S HAVE THE DANCE NEXT WEEK!
THAT'S A GREAT IDEA, ARCHIE!
THEN BETTY WILL BE ABLE TO COME!
TO DO
DE RATIONS

I'LL TALK TO MR. WEATHERBEE AND IF HE GIVES THE OKAY, THEN NEXT WEEK WE PARTY!

AND SOON...
MR. BEE AGREES!
COOL! NOW HERE'S THE GUEST LIST!
6

IF EVERYBODY TELLS TEN PEOPLE THE DANCE IS OFF, THEN NO ONE WILL SHOW UP!
GIVE ME MY TEN!
LET'S GET MOVIN'!
WE GOTTA SPREAD THE WORD!

AND SOON...
HEY, JUGHEAD! HAVE YOU SEEN VERONICA?
CAN'T SAY I HAVE, OL' BUDDY!
I'VE TALKED TO ALL THE NAMES ON MY LIST *EXCEPT* RONNIE!
ALL MY NAMES ARE RIGHT HERE!
DID YOU HEAR?
YEAH!
BETTY'S GOT THE FLU!

MR. LODGE SAID SHE AND SMITHERS LEFT HOURS AGO AND RONNIE DEMANDED NOT TO BE *DISTURBED* NO MATTER WHAT!
DON'T WORRY, ARCH! SHE'S PROBABLY HEARD THE NEWS BY NOW...

EVERYBODY ELSE HAS!
I GUESS YOU'RE RIGHT, JUGHEAD!
NO PARTY TONIGHT!
POP'S
BOO HOO!
7

MEANWHILE...
AHHH, YES! I'VE GOT THE PERFECT DRESS FOR MY GRAND ENTRANCE!
The Exclusive
The Exclusive

AND NOW ONTO "LOUIS MICHAEL'S SALON," SMITHERS!
YES, MS. LODGE!
The Exclusive
La Chic

AND SOON...
THIS IS IT! THE HAIRSTYLE FOR MY GRAND ENTRANCE!

NOW I VIL' MAKE UP YOUR BEAUTIFUL VACE, AND OOH LA LA!

BRITNEY, STEP ASIDE! HERE COMES ZE VON AND ONLY... VERONICA LODGE!
8

AND NOW ON TO RIVERDALE, SMITHERS!
YES, MS. LODGE!
LODGE
I'M AN HOUR LATE! THE PERFECT TIME FOR MY ENTRANCE!

RIVERDA
HMMM... THAT'S STRANGE... I DON'T HEAR ANY MUSIC FROM THE GYM...

I GUESS THEY'RE ALL WAITING FOR ME TO BEGIN!

WELL... THIS IS IT!
9

PLOP!
ARE YOU OKAY?
I'M FINE! BUT WHERE'S THE DANCE?
POSTPONED UNTIL NEXT VEEK!
BETTY COOPER GOT SICK AND NO ONE VANTED TO HAVE THE DANCE VITHOUT HER!
AHHHHHHHHH!
VAS IT SOMETHING I SAID?
THE END

Art: Dan Parent

Originally printed in BETTY & VERONICA SPECTACULAR #26, NOVEMBER 1997

Story: George Gladir   Pencils: Stan Goldberg
Inks: Rudy Lapick   Letters: Bill Yoshida

Originally printed in BETTY & VERONICA SPECTACULAR #26, NOVEMBER 1997

Story: George Gladir Pencils: Stan Goldberg
Inks: Mike Esposito Letters: Bill Yoshida

Originally printed in BETTY & VERONICA SPECTACULAR #26, NOVEMBER 1997

Story & Pencils: Dan Parent

Inks: Jon D'Agostino Letters: Bill Yoshida Colors: Barry Grossman

Originally printed in BETTY & VERONICA SPECTACULAR #26, NOVEMBER 1997

ER--ISN'T HE A BIT RAMBUNCTIOUS FOR YOU TO HANDLE?
YES! BUT HE'S THE ONLY YOUNG PERSON I KNOW!

SO...
JENNIFER, HOW HAS BETTY POSITIVELY AFFECTED YOUR LIFE?
SHE HELPED TUTOR ME IN GEOGRAPHY!
Bring A Young Friend To School Day!

MY GRADE HAS GONE FROM A "C" TO AN "A"!
MARVELOUS! THAT'S OUR BETTY!

AND LEROY! HOW HAS VERONICA AFFECTED YOUR LIFE?
EASY! SHE GAVE ME 50 BUCKS TO COME HERE TODAY!

SHE PAID YOU?
AND SOMETIMES SHE PAYS ME TO STAY OUT OF HER HAIR!

VERONICA! QUICK PAYOFFS AREN'T GOING TO HELP HIM!
SPEND TIME WITH HIM! DEVELOP A HOBBY WITH HIM! BE A MENTOR!
2

I'LL GIVE YOU A COUPLE OF WEEKS TO REASSESS THIS PROJECT!
OH, GREAT! NOW WE *HAVE* TO BOND!!
WHAT A DRAG!
SO...
HAVE YOU AND LEROY BEEN BONDING?
ACTUALLY, YES! HE'S SHOWN AN INTEREST IN PHOTOGRAPHY!

AND YOU *LOVE* TO BE *PHOTOGRAPHED*!
WHAT A *MATCH* MADE IN HEAVEN!

YOU CAN PHOTOGRAPH ME IN MY NEW FALL *WARDROBE*!
OKAY, COUSIN!
WELL, IT IS SORT OF PROMISING, IN A *VAIN* SORT OF WAY!

SO...
WHAT HAVE YOU *TWO* BEEN UP TO?
LEROY HAS TAKEN AN INTEREST IN *PHOTOGRAPHY*!

OKAY! THAT SOUNDS *INTERESTING*!
HERE'S SOME SHOTS OF HIS WORK! NOT BAD, HUH?
3

I'VE GOT SOME OTHER PICTURES TOO, COUSIN!
OH? WHAT DO YOU MEAN?
GAK! YOU TOOK ONE OF ME SLEEPING!
AND MY, HOW YOU DO SNORE!
AND THERE'S YOU WITH ALL YOUR BEAUTY PREPARATIONS!
THIS SHOT WAS EASY WITH THE TWO-WAY MIRROR I REPLACED YOUR OLD ONE WITH!
HYUCK! HYUCK
HA! HA!
HAR! HAR!
WHY ARE YOU DOING THIS?
I'M A PRECOCIOUS LITTLE BOY! PLUS, I FIGURE YOU'LL PAY ME BIG BUCKS NOT TO SHOW THESE...
GAK!! PHOTOS OF ME LIP-SYNCING IN FRONT OF MY MIRROR! I LOOK RIDICULOUS!
HOW MUCH IS THIS WORTH NOT TO SHOW?
TONIGHT'S HOMEWORK
HOW ABOUT YOUR LIFE?!
HELP! HELP!
4

VERONICA! LEROY! STOP THIS NONSENSE!
YOU BOTH ACT LIKE 5-YEAR-OLDS! AND THAT'S AN INSULT TO 5-YEAR-OLDS EVERYWHERE!

YOU'VE FAILED THIS PROJECT, VERONICA!
GIVE US ONE MORE CHANCE! I HAVE AN IDEA!

OH, ALL RIGHT! I'M A GLUTTON FOR PUNISHMENT!
BETTY, YOU'VE GOT TO HELP ME...
HONOR ROLL
A WEEK LATER...
SO, VERONICA! HOW ARE YOU MOLDING HIS YOUNG MIND?
ASK BETTY! I'VE PUT HER IN CHARGE OF LEROY...

BUT HOW DOES THAT POSITIVELY AFFECT LEROY?
EASY! BETTY'S A MUCH BETTER INFLUENCE THAN I AM!

THEREFORE, I'VE POSITIVELY AFFECTED THE BOY!
YOU KNOW, I HATE TO ADMIT IT, BUT SHE'S GOT SOMETHING THERE!
END

Story: Kathleen Webb Pencils: Dan Parent
Inks: Jon D'Agostino Letters: Bill Yoshida Colors: Barry Grossman

Originally printed in BETTY & VERONICA SPECTACULAR #26, NOVEMBER 1997

HEY, RON! THROW YOURSELF IN TO HELP AND I MIGHT BID 50 BUCKS!
OH, YEAH ?!?
EXIT
ALL RIGHT, MR. MONEYBAGS, YOU'VE GOT YOURSELF A DEAL!
SOLD TO REGGIE MANTLE FOR 50 BUCKS!
?

AND HOW ABOUT THE REST OF YOU LOWLIFES? WE CAN WASH MORE THAN ONE CAR! COME ON!
ER...RON...

HOW ABOUT MINE? I CAN AFFORD $25!
SOLD TO MICHAEL RAY FOR $25!

AM I A GREAT AUCTIONEER, OR WHAT? I RAISED SEVENTY-FIVE DOLLARS FOR A CAUSE!
YOU ALSO GOT US JOBS WITH RIVERDALE'S BIGGEST WOLVES!

OH, PISH POSH! I CAN HANDLE BOTH OF THEM!
YOU'LL HAVE TO! MEET YOU TOMORROW AT REGGIE'S! TEN A.M. SHARP!
2

SOOOO...THE NEXT MORNING, AT TEN A.M....
I WISH I DIDN'T HAVE TO GIVE UP A SATURDAY TO DO THIS ... OH, WELL...
HI, BETS!
WHERE'S YOUR CHARMING PARTNER?
SHE SHOULD BE ALONG ANY MINUTE! I'LL GET STARTED!
THIS IS RIDICULOUS! I'M ALMOST FINISHED, AND STILL NO RON!
WHERE ON EARTH...
HE-LLOOO...
SORRY IT TOOK ME SO LONG TO GET HERE, BUT I HAD SUCH TROUBLE FINDING THE PERFECT OUTFIT!
WHAT'S TO WEAR? JEANS AND A T-SHIRT!
WANT SOME LEMONADE AND COOKIES FOR ALL YOUR HARD LABOR?
I CAN USE A BREAK!
YOU'VE ONLY BEEN HERE TEN MINUTES!
LOVE THE WAY YOU HANDLE THAT POLISHING CLOTH, RON!
THANKS! YOU MISSED A SPOT, BETTY DEAR!
GRRRRRR!
3

NOW THAT "WE" ARE DONE, "WE" SHOULD HEAD OVER TO MICHAEL'S, RON!
SEE YOU LATER, REGGIE!
`BYE!

SHE'S ALL YOURS, GIRLS!
WE'LL MAKE YOU PROUD OF HER, MICHAEL!

YOU WANT TO RUN THE HOSE, RON, OR USE THE SPONGE?
NEITHER!

THAT FILTHY CAR WILL RUIN MY DESIGNER CLOTHES!
I'LL SUPERVISE YOUR WORK!

YOU GOT US THESE JOBS, NOW YOU'RE GOING TO HELP!
OR I WILL TURN THIS HOSE ON YOU!!
YOU WOULDN'T!
TRY ME!
OH, ALL RIGHT! I'LL RUN THE HOSE! YOU SPONGE DOWN THE CAR!
4

HOW'S IT GOING, CUTIES?
IT'S STRENUOUS WORK, MICHAEL, DARLING!
YOU'VE DONE A SUPERB JOB, RON! HOW ABOUT A DATE THIS SATURDAY?
(GIGGLE) I'LL GIVE IT SOME THOUGHT!
ALMOST DONE, BETTY?
NO! NO THANKS TO YOU! ARE YOU GOING TO DO YOUR PART OR AREN'T YOU?!
I HAVE BEEN! I SAID I'D HANDLE REGGIE AND MICHAEL DIDN'T I?
AND YOU'VE MISSED THE SAME SPOT AGAIN!
OH? WELL...
SPLOOSH
?
THIS TIME I GOT IT!!
END

Art: Dan Parent

Originally printed in BETTY & VERONICA SPECTACULAR #27, JANUARY 1998